Books in

The Human-Hybrid Project

series:

The Russian's Revenge

The Russian's Revenge

Farley L. Dunn

THREE SKILLET

Published in Fort Worth, Texas

 THREE SKILLET

www.ThreeSkilletPublishing.com

Three Skillet Publishing
PO Box 162194
Fort Worth, Texas 76161

ISBN: 978-1-957173-09-2

Printed in the USA

The Russian's Revenge

— Book 10 —

The Human-Hybrid Project

Corona Tower Research Complex

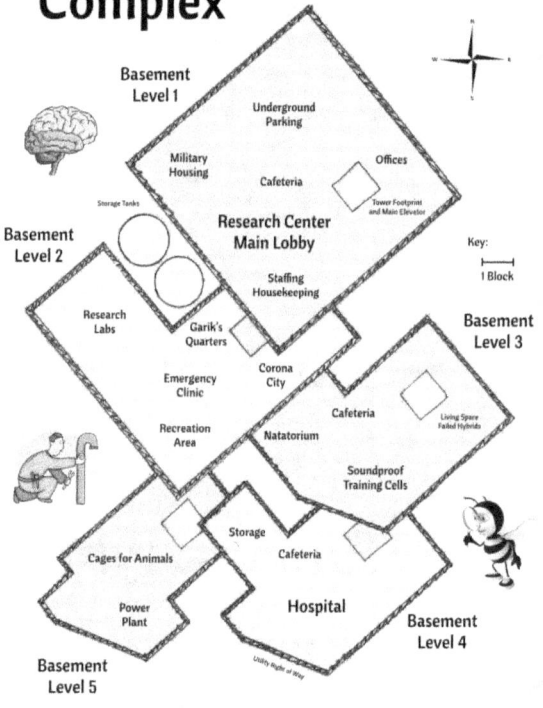

Basement Level 1

Underground Parking

Military Housing

Offices

Cafeteria

Tower Footprint and Main Elevator

Storage Tanks

Research Center Main Lobby

Basement Level 2

Staffing Housekeeping

Key:
⊢——⊣
1 Block

Research Labs

Garik's Quarters

Basement Level 3

Emergency Clinic

Corona City

Recreation Area

Cafeteria

Living Space Failed Hybrids

Natatorium

Soundproof Training Cells

Storage

Cafeteria

Cages for Animals

Hospital

Basement Level 4

Power Plant

Utility Right of Way

Basement Level 5

Corona Tower
Your Home Away from Home

**Penthouse Level
40th Floor**

Weston Rodheimer's
Penthouse Suite

Halo Sunchaser's
Apartment

Floor 7

Stamford Suites
Grill, Pool
and Gym

Jantzen Hefferly/
Garik Shayk's
Apartment

Floors 2-6

Stamford Suites
Hotel and
Apartments

First Floor

Lobby and
Glass-Walled
Atrium

**Open to
the Mall**

Chow Down and
the Elevator Entrance
to the Rest of the
Tower

$$- I -$$

arik Shayk, survivor.

Well, sort of. If being the lone human hybrid remaining in the Corona Tower research facility counted as surviving ... when they were about to remove his spinal fluid to enhance three hundred super soldiers and make them just like him, only more compliant to their demands ... and didn't have intentions for him to survive the procedure.

He watched Dr. Jamie Jimenez move about the equipment-lined room in his white lab coat, checking readouts, adjusting several, at one point pulling a keyboard to him and adding information to a digital chart visible on the display.

"Canada, huh, Dr. Jamie?" Garik called to the man's back. Jimenez headed the hospital on Basement Level 4 of the underground research complex. Using the man's first name would appeal to his vanity. He liked to think of himself as a patient's doctor, a friend, even if the veneer was paper thin. "The Director said the new Canadian facility is open, so that must be where everyone is, right? It must be quite a place to absorb everyone from here."

"Yes." Jimenez paused in his busy activities and turned to Garik on the table, his arms and legs strapped firmly down with metal clamps. Satisfied he would not be in any danger, he approached. "I see you have come to terms with your situation. We do not wish you to suffer more than necessary. Your willing compliance will further our goals with the least disruption possible. And while we are waiting to move ahead, you will be given the best of care. We are not cruel. We want this to be easy for everyone with no further glitches."

The glitch in the process for Garik was that they needed to use his cranial-spinal fluid to concentrate the DNA enough to bring about the required hybrid adaptations in the three hundred new volunteers.

All of it, leaving him none.

"Three hundred, right?" Garik forced himself to

show outward compliance. Inwardly, he burned. *It's my spinal fluid, and I'm supposed to have accepted my situation?* He pulled at the metal clamps. Even with his new levels of hybridized strength, they didn't budge.

"It is what the Director requested. I suppose we have you to thank for this leap forward." Jimenez moved closer to Garik and looked him over. He touched the clamp at one wrist, as if making sure it was secure. "Your theft of the sword so infuriated Halo that she forbade further research. Are we ready? Perhaps." He chuckled. "She hopes you to be our confirmation."

"I guess I would be proud to have helped out," Garik kept his voice level, but containing his anger was hard, "if I had actually stolen it."

After the alleged theft of Halo Sunchaser's electrified sword, the secretive underground Bay City research facility was emptied as Garik remained in isolation for two weeks in one of the penthouse apartments in the 40-story Tower. Garik knew very little, except that they considered his timber-wolf-and-human-hybrid mix to be the ultimate in DNA melding, and they planned to harvest his DNA to begin building a new level of soldier that could intermingle with normal humans yet disguise the skills that made them superhuman.

"Denials reflect a poor attitude. Not a good reflection on your change of heart, Mr. Shayk." Jimenez seemed to lose interest in the conversation. He only wanted compliance, not truth, and he stepped away.

Garik heard the use of his last name, a demotion, a black mark from Jimenez dropping him to the bottom of the doctor's value meter. He remembered an apology he gave Jimenez once, groveling to play the man's emotions to help save a fellow hybrid. The man had been lost, anyway. Garik would not grovel now.

Memories swept through him, flooding him with emotions. Jantzen Hefferly, his mentor and father figure, lost to the sword. Paul Gberie and John Carter, left for dead on the parking garage floor. Stephen Klandermans, Jacquelien Van Kessel, Fabiola Bello, ripped up by the roots and likely transplanted in far-off Canada. Giselle Harmon, Paolo Leveen, Julia Cantos, broken by Sunchaser's electrically produced sonic boom. His girlfriend, Marisa Bruni, killed by the sword to trigger his final metamorphosis into his true hybrid form.

If this *was* his final form, eight inches taller, enlarged lung capacity, and a heart three times its normal size; and that didn't touch the things that couldn't be easily measured: his eyeshine; his capacity to read a scene from surrounding aromas; his hearing, more sensitive than even Jimenez could imagine.

And the rainbows . . . his ability to move so quickly that time seemed to stand still, blurring the world into shimmering layers of refracted light—rainbows—and letting him do amazing things, all for about half a minute before it drained his body and left him exhausted and on the floor.

Restrained on the table, he gave in to his anger, and the room came to a standstill around him. Rainbows burst from every surface, the swirling refraction of oil on water, a dark, slick coating that made Dr. Jimenez and the machines and the room all blur together. The doctor held out a hand to a button, frozen, and the display at its side was in a half-on-half-off state, making it hard to read. The light overhead pulsed with a ring of colors, a full 360-degree waterfall of rainbow brilliance. Garik studied the metal rainbows at his wrists. He pulled, lifted, strained; twisted his wrists, compressed one hand, was even certain he broke a bone that healed too quickly for him to force his hand through the loop.

Another side effect of his DNA transformation: healing so rapidly that the knitting process was visible to the eye, with bone and skin reforming as you watched.

He wrestled and wrenched against his bonds, certain he could free himself. If only he were Jantzen, able to sublimate—morph—from solid to gas, he would be free and out of here.

Then his half minute was up, his resources were drained, and his anger was sliced from him, slumping to the floor in a crumpled heap, leaving him panting with exhaustion.

"Now, now, Mr. Shayk. We have pressure sensors

on your restraints. No need to prove something everyone agrees you cannot do."

The man didn't even look at Garik when he spoke to him. It told one thing. They didn't know about the rainbows, about how fast he could move, even if it was only for a short time. He tried to formulate a plan, a way to get out of these cuffs and onto his feet. Out of this room. Exit this place so fast they wouldn't know he was gone until he was halfway across the world.

Houdini himself to a better place, one that had never heard of Corona Tower, Weston Rodheimer, or Halo Sunchaser.

The black god of exhaustion got the better of him. It swooped down like a bird, the heavens raining fire, a praying mantis with Popeye arms divided by extra joints in the forearms, one named Justin Kurtew, a man he used to know.

Used to know because Justin was now more mantis than man, hardly human at all.

As the darkness ate him up, Garik felt his hackles rise, and deep within him, his reasoning faded, a growl that was a basso rumble formed at the back of his throat, and he lifted his head and howled.

The sound was his need for revenge for all that he had lost. It was out there, and it would be his.

Then he collapsed into embers and ash, and the blackness of oblivion swallowed him whole.

DAY ONE, two, or three? Garik didn't know. He had pulled at the restraints several times, on each occasion felled by the ash god of oblivion. This time when he woke, he had a tube in his arm, and above him bags of energy leaked life into his veins.

"I would prefer pizza," he called into the room.

"Good, you're awake." Nurse Leah Fortinier walked from behind him into his line of sight. She reached to the bag, squeezed it gently, then pulled a marker from her pocket. She neatly printed *pizza* on the bag. "There, taste better?"

"Absolutely. I'm glad to see you've developed a sense of humor."

"I've always had a sense of humor. You've just failed to appreciate it."

"Tell me about Canada. Please."

"Please? Did I hear you correctly?" She stopped as if surprised.

"I'm appealing to your sense of humor. If I make you laugh, you might answer my question. Canada, please?"

"Certainly. It lies mostly above the forty-ninth parallel north, is the second largest country in the world, and holds over half of all the lakes in existence. There are two official languages—"

"Thank you, Coach Cates. He was my sixth-grade geography teacher, if you're asking, and he was more thorough than I wanted him to be. So, I know all that.

Tell me about the Canadian research facility. How's it like this? Different, too?"

"Does it matter?" She pulled back the lapels of his pajamas and attached two sensors to his chest with sticky pads.

"I've got nothing else to do but listen." It hit him that he hadn't been wearing pajamas when he was first locked into the restraints. "The pajamas. How did you do that?"

"I didn't." She smiled. She worked another sensor under his pajama leg to the top of his thigh, and then produced two more for the inside of each elbow. "You must sleep sometime. We, meaning the hospital staff, took advantage."

"I hope not," he mumbled.

"Hope not what?" She worked the wires on the various sensors to a panel at the foot of the bed and began plugging them in.

"Nothing. If I slept, it's been a day at least. Correct?" Colonel Brace had said he would have his "volunteers" on site within three days. If Garik was to survive this, he had to come up with a plan, one that didn't include his brain and spinal juices being sucked from his body to enable three hundred soldiers to become DNA clones of him.

Why did being perfect—according to Director Rodheimer—have to be so difficult?

GARIK LEARNED to tell who walked into the room before he opened his eyes. Artificially applied scents, natural pheromones, even people's preferred hand soap. His ears told him nearly as much. Nurse Fortinier walked with a hard heel-first step, very precise and businesslike. Dr. Jimenez was softer, almost creeping, as though he wanted to observe without being observed. Brace had been in once, standing behind Garik, telling Jimenez in a low voice that the Canadians had a much more modern facility, and he could arrange for him to be transferred with a word. Garik recognized the man's smell before he began to speak.

"The city, Colonel. Can you offer me that?"

"Yellowknife is only an hour by plane. Anything you need, and I mean anything, can be shipped in for your convenience."

"And who would watch over your three hundred volunteers, Colonel? They must have the best care possible, and that is me."

"I am working on that. We have begun eliminating—"

Garik stopped listening at that point. *Eliminating!* Brace was referencing people he knew. He had studied the methods of Nazi Germany and the prison camps of the war. Experiment on people the rest of the world doesn't know or care about, and when you have used them up, eliminate them. The Nazis had used guns, gas, and ovens. The Tower had repurposed the hybrid failures for a living DNA bank, and once they had what they needed, they harvested reusable body parts. He remembered Chad Sherwin's legs, "donated" by another hybrid that couldn't use them.

Harvested was more like it.

"Are you sure the creature can't hear us?" Brace's words brought Garik back into the room.

"He is a man, Colonel, and he is sleeping."

"Those needles moved."

Garik didn't know the needles they were watching, but he forced his breathing and heart into a sleep-like rhythm. Slower, slower. He could do this.

"See, Colonel? Just dreaming. Everything has settled down. About Canada. Ask me again when we have your men fully hybridized. I might be agreeable."

Garik's anger was a rising storm. *Eliminating. I don't think so, Colonel Brace, not as I live and breathe.* Man or wolf, he would do whatever it took to get to his friends.

He locked onto one thing: Yellowknife. Then a second: one hour away.

That's where his pack was, and an alpha wolf never abandons the pack.

— 2 —

n invasion of suits and uniforms paraded through the door. They didn't ask and Garik couldn't have refused with his limbs firmly embedded into restraints that seemed stronger than steel.

"Am I the guest of honor?" Garik felt his situation like a vice, about to squeeze him in two. These people were the pinchers on one side, and his impending brain drain was on the other. They were coming together, and he was caught in the middle.

"As you will note, gentlemen, no dulling of mental

sharpness or wit." Weston Rodheimer, with his broad shoulders derived from his silverback gorilla DNA, let the words rumble from him.

"This is our Action Plan?" Lt. Col. Marjorie Fair, wearing red hair and a dense pattern of freckles, looked doubtful. "Alfred, give us your input."

"Yes, ma'am." Major Alfred Lipstitch stepped forward. Tightly groomed dark hair told of his desire for perfection, to keep the program moving forward to complete and utter success. "First note, the men will not react well to the restraints on the prototype. They must be removed."

"I agree, Director." Fair. "We are under the oversight of Community Service, even within the auspices of this program. The well-being of each volunteer is at the heart of team morale."

"Brace?" Rodheimer by-stepped formalities and cut his question directly to the colonel. "We have consistently operated independently of oversight. Otherwise, we cannot successfully move forward."

"I understand, Director. Washington gives me no leeway in this." Colonel William Brace, a man with pretentions to Southern gentility, seemed almost apologetic.

"This is a new policy?" Rodheimer's words were hard.

"Not at all, Director. Your previous volunteers—" meaning everyone recently relocated to the new Canadian facility, "—were civilians or otherwise outside the U.S. military infrastructure. You have requested three hundred of our finest enlisted—"

"And this is different than the team we provided you with previously? They required no such Community Service." Rodheimer referenced the flawed paramilitary goons Brace had used to wrest control of Corona Tower from the Director when the power structure in Bay City had nearly collapsed under the weight of public protests, rioting, and terrorist activity. Brace's "goons" required oxygen concentrators to supplement their bodies' oxygen consumption during military exercises. They were frighteningly capable but flawed, and Garik was the pivot for creating the improved super soldier that would revolutionize military machines around the world.

"Ma'am, if I may." Lipstitch stepped forward slightly. "Director Rodheimer, the first team to be hybridized had the government's assurance that this was a tested and approved procedure with no possibility of side effects. But as you know—"

"Dr. Jamie," Rodheimer interrupted, now fully irritated, "please explain to this man that we gave them flawed men because Colonel Brace insisted that we come through with product. Rushed product. Incomplete product. This falls on the military's shoulders, not ours."

"Unimportant," Lipstitch said, brushing the interruption aside. "The first team entered this program with wide eyes expecting no issues. That's not what they got. This new team has seen the drawbacks of the first team's DNA enhancement. They have requested assurance that they will not suffer a similar drawback."

"Thank you, Alfred," Fair said. "And that is where Community Service comes into play. The men who have already arrived wish to meet with the prototype, see that he is fully functional, perhaps view his skills in action. The others on the way will likely have the same request."

"Director, is this possible?" Brace asked his question in a tone that indicated it had better be.

"Let me see what I can work out. The, um, *prototype* is our singular example, and to replicate the DNA melding process in a new prototype . . . I will have to work out how to meet your request without jeopardizing our end goals."

"Understood. Thank you, Director." Fair looked to Brace and Lipstitch. "We are through here? I have other duties on my plate. If I have your permission, Colonel?"

Garik watched the military fluffs file out, never having spoken to him or responded to his question, no more than a cipher in their day, a prototype to use up and discard at will.

As Rodheimer reached the door, he turned to study Garik, looked to Jimenez and nodded, then faced forward and was gone.

"Was I the guest of honor?" He prodded Jimenez, hoping to get him to acknowledge him as a real person.

"If you wish," the doctor said. He looked hard at Garik, evaluating, and not kindly. "If we must do as requested, there can be no errors. No escapes, no independent action. We will preview a plan, and we will stick to it. I hope that's clear."

"Clear," Garik said. The man nodded and moved away. He still hadn't used Garik's name, either first or last. And *prototype?* Whatever plan Jimenez and Rodheimer put into place, they might intend to stick to it, but Garik had other ideas. His hero, Harry Houdini, had been able to escape anything. Now it was Garik's turn, and he let the problem ping about in his brain. There was nothing else to do. He was strapped onto a table, again with fresh clothes, once again taken advantage of during the night. He suspected Nurse Ratchett's sleepy juice was involved. Otherwise, he would have noticed, you'd think, someone manhandling him to change his clothes. One thought rankled more than all the rest. *It was likely to happen again,* with or without his permission. He twisted his arms under his restraints, trying to force them free, only to admit he was trapped until he came up with a plan.

MORE SHACKLES, of a different sort, the kind with minders carrying dart pistols, as Garik was released to dress for the meet-and-greet with the men he would be sharing his LIFE WITH.

"Privacy? Or am I no longer allowed that?" Garik held the clothes he'd been given, a lightweight black turtleneck with long sleeves, gray slacks, polished black brogues, and socks and boxer briefs. Even a stick of deodorant. A belt was coiled and in one of the shoes. He recognized the things from his closet and knew they'd gone through everything he owned.

"I'm afraid not." Second Lt. Ron Wilder, a man with thinning hair and delicate features. His arms looked like they could bust bricks. "You may stand behind the chair if you feel the need."

Wilder held his hand just over the butt of his holstered gun, prepared, prepared. Something about the way he stood was off, and Garik let the image work through him as he stepped behind the chair and began to work his "lock-up" things off and kicked them to the side before selecting the briefs. He slipped them on, watching Wilder, and his memory linked a documentary he'd once watched about Israeli agents who'd hunted down Nazis in hiding after the war. Then another with real Mossad agents telling their story of pursuing the terrorist group Black September after they had killed eleven members of the Israeli Olympic team in Munich in the 70s.

The gears clicked, and Garik wondered if Colonel Brace knew one of his men was Mossad, likely with a degree from Harvard, a family on Long Island, adored nieces and nephews, and even pictures of them—all fictional. That's how it worked in the world of undercover.

Surely the man wasn't also hybrid. With those arms . . . was it possible that Israel had a program of their own, and Wilder was here to ensure that North America didn't best them at their own game?

Garik slipped his shirt over his head, his arms through the sleeves, his eyes back on Wilder. They had met for the first time in the elevator. Airman Vang had been present, and Vang and Wilder had teamed up against him. A diversion? Garik had only seen him once more with Vang, never noticed him in a routine or even in the same location, and the man had pretended not to recognize Garik the last time they'd met.

The only thing Garik hadn't observed was the man slitting his plastic trash bags so his garbage couldn't be stolen from a dumpster. He smiled at that.

"Something amusing, Mr. Shayk?"

"Just picturing you cutting up your trash bags before dropping them in a dumpster."

"That's an odd thing to say." Wilder's hand lowered to his weapon, and his eyes narrowed.

"Only if you're—" Garik glanced at the two minders with the dart guns. They were trained on him.

"Only what, Mr. Shayk?"

"Only if you're a neat freak. Then it would be odd."

Garik shrugged and he moved to the other side of the chair to sit and put on his shoes.

Wilder's hand relaxed, and he motioned to the two men with him. "He's ready. Shackles on, then let's move toward the training area."

Garik groaned. The men pulled out metal shackles that they fastened to his wrists and his ankles, with a chain connecting them.

"You've got to be kidding me."

"Director's orders." Wilder pulled a key from his pocket and showed it to Garik. "I have the only one, and it's right here."

"Won't the new volunteers see the chains?" He pulled his arms up as high as possible and shook them.

"Once we're on the elevator, the building will go into lockdown. Only my passkey will still permit movement around the facility. Remember that, Mr. Shayk, only my passkey. You will be released then. Not before."

"Small favors," Garik mumbled.

"Perhaps not so small," Wilder assured him, and they headed out the door, with Garik nearly tripping with every step he took.

ABOUT thirty men were gathered in the recreation area, this first group having flown in directly from the Canadian facility. When they arrived, a number were looking around, inspecting the amenities. Others were seated, bored, waiting on the display of Garik's skills to start. They carried a cross section of the world in their faces, many in bronze or coffee shades. The pale, blond faces were the fewest. Most were unlined, a few more mature, but all trim and fit.

A good thing, Garik considered, a leg up for those aspiring to become an improvement to what Colonel Brace's paramilitary already were.

Garik's arrival with Wilder changed the tone of the room. Men tapped shoulders, pointed, whispered, called to their friends, shifted chairs, moved to sit closer to the front. Garik realized he must present an appealing sight. Six-four, a thick chest, and powerful legs. What military man wouldn't wish to tower over almost everyone around him?

Wilder introduced him, asked them to hold off on their questions about his abilities, that Garik would provide some demonstrations later. Now was their time to find out about his experience going through the transformation. He directed Garik to a seat in front of the men, and he opened the floor for questions. The two dart guns, concealed from the crowd, were at his back.

The first question was from a blond man with buzzed hair. "We've seen some of the hybrids. Does the process hurt?"

"Only if you don't request sleepy juice," Garik responded. He heard chuckles in the crowd.

"Will we look like you after we change?" A coffee

man with tight hair painted on his head. The implication was *or something weird like them?*

"Only if you want to become better looking." Garik grinned.

The questions began to come faster, from the length of time it had taken Garik to change, to the accommodations they could expect in the facility.

It was as they were moving toward the demonstration area that Garik overheard someone whisper, "Do you think he knows the guy with the purple eyes?"

"Who asked that?" He stopped and looked over the men, narrowing it down to one area. Three men were walking side by side.

"You could hear that?" The man was surprised.

"You said *knows*. What man with purple eyes?"

"Tim-o, you've met him. What's his name?"

"Hefferly, I think. Yeah, Jantzen Hefferly."

"He's alive?" Garik felt the floor rise up and hit him in the chest.

"Last time I checked," the man said, "and that was two days ago."

For Garik, this changed everything.

robabilities swam before Garik.

Rodheimer would call it prescience, even precognition, but it was neither. Garik observed, evaluated, and extrapolated. He followed the lines of probabilities until they were exhausted, understanding that choosing one altered all the others.

Even seeing the probabilities changed how he reacted to them, and that was another facet he had to consider.

Jantzen, able to morph—or sublimate—directly

from a solid into purple smoke—a gas—and resolidify at will, a derivative of his squid DNA, was unique even among the human hybrids that had come out of the secretive basement research center underneath Corona Tower. How could he be alive? The sword . . . it was the only possibility.

Garik had located the final layer of the missing schematics and determined that the arcing lightning that spat from the end was due to a short in the system, an incomplete part of the design, a flaw intentionally incorporated into the prototype device for some reason of Halo Sunchaser's. With the final page of the schematics, Garik had intuited that the original design was some sort of conduit.

A mechanized teleportation device? The idea boggled his mind, but if Jantzen was in Canada after Garik had watched the electrical jolt from the sword slam into him and dismantle him molecule by molecule, atom by atom . . .

And that's when his mind put it together. That's exactly what the sword had done, disassembled Jantzen atom by atom, and he had been reassembled elsewhere. The obvious answer was the new Canadian facility.

Sublimation to the extreme. The ultimate process of shifting directly from a solid to a gas. Transferring to some sort of energy wave that could be reconstituted a thousand or two miles away.

What a coup this would be for Sunchaser and

Rodheimer. No wonder they had disguised it from Colonel Brace and hidden the only copy of the final layer of the schematics in a secured room deep within the research facility. Moving weapons, troops, whatever they needed directly from one location to another. Even space travel, eliminating the need to lift every pound of supplies on rocket ships. Reassemble it from the surface of the planet directly onto an orbital station.

Any nation would pay an exorbitant fee to gain access to such game-changing technology.

Garik processed his revelation with one part of his mind, while his body exhibited his super-human, wolf-infused abilities to the men who had come to see the Tower's tame wolf perform. His fist, splitting a punching bag with one blow. Wrestling one of their strongest and laying him to the mat with ease. Lights down and still seeing like it was daylight. A level of flexibility that enabled him to force his body through confining mazes. Even stripping to a suit and entering the pool . . . five minutes . . . ten . . . fifteen, until he was asked to come up. He also got to show them the difficulty of clearing his lungs of pool water when he needed to breathe air once again.

All the time half of his mind was focused on Jantzen . . . alive . . . and in Canada. He had to get there, to Houdini out of this place, to . . . to do what, he didn't know. But it was Jantzen! He was alive!

At the end of his demonstration, still wearing his

suit and his towel over one shoulder, he called to the man who said he'd met Jantzen.

"Tim-o, wait up!" He waved a hand, lifted the towel and rubbed it over his hair, and stepped his direction. He was stopped by one of the minders with the dart gun no one could see.

"Not so far, Shayk," the man growled.

"Mr. Shayk to you," Garik retorted. "Or use my first name. I'm not going anywhere. I understand my situation." Lockdown. Dart guns. They had all the power, and once again, like his entire life, he had none at all. "I just want to talk to the man."

"Okay, then." The minder gave a little bit, just enough for Garik to greet the man.

"Tim-o," Garik said, holding out a hand to shake. "Thanks for talking to me."

"It's Tim. Shane's a dork. All that was impressive. I'm looking forward to this. I suppose you'll be training us, you know, since you've gone through this. It takes an expert to make an expert." Tim smiled, open and friendly.

"Maybe." Actually not, especially as he would be DEAD. But that revelation wasn't why he had called the man over. "You said you'd seen Jantzen Hefferly."

"Sure. What do you want to know?"

"Um, anything. How long's he been there? How did he arrive? How's he doing?" Did he ask about me? Did he send a message? Does he remember that I'm still here and care that I'm about to have my brain-juices sucked out and given to you people?

"I don't know about most of that. Sorry." Tim shrugged. "We know him because of his purple eyes, the only person I've ever seen like that."

"What's he doing there?"

"That I can answer. Not much. He's a space cadet, a zombie, an airhead—"

"Sure. I get it." Garik didn't, though. Jantzen was brilliant.

"I don't mean to offend, but he blanks out. That's when the purple eyes really shine. We like to talk to him just to watch it happen."

"Enough." The minder stepped closer. "Mr. Shayk, Lt. Wilder is signaling it's time."

"Thank you, Tim." Garik nodded.

"Anytime. Request me for training. I want on your team."

Garik smiled and nodded. They hadn't told these men that someone had to die for them to become super soldiers. No surprise there. Especially as they weren't the ones that had to do the dying part.

BACK AT the elevator, Wilder inserted his passkey to open the doors, then inside, he inserted it once again to close them. He didn't set a location but stepped out of the way as the minders with the dart guns pulled out the manacles and chains.

"Still can't trust me, huh?" And for good reason, Garik thought. Houdini, Houdini. It was the only thing on his mind, except that Jantzen was alive!

"The building is in lockdown. You do know what that means." Wilder stepped to the side as the two minders sorted out the restraints.

"Yes, yes, and only your passkey moves the elevator." When the man started to withdraw his key to the manacles, Garik tilted his head, rolled his eyes, and said, "And you have the only key to my freedom. I get it. I have no power at all, and I might as well get used to it."

"I'm glad to see you listen well."

The men had Garik's legs and one arm locked in, and one held his other wrist, preparing to latch it, when Wilder drew a third dart gun from inside his jacket, aimed it at the neck of the man to Garik's right and fired. Then, before the man to Garik's left could look up, he turned the dart gun and took him out, too.

Wilder put his finger to his lips, and he withdrew a cloth from a sealed bag, knelt, and held it over the men's noses until they passed out.

"My turn?" Garik could likely take the man, even with only one free hand, but the passkey was a bigger problem. Without Wilder's thumbprint, it wasn't taking him very far.

"Your turn?" Wilder stood. "Perhaps, but not the way you think. The dart is a muscle relaxant, only. I need them to not remember. The pad will blur the events just before and after. You. You said you remember what I told you?"

"Sure. I don't forget." Since his change into part werewolf, he couldn't forget, visual or auditory. Eidetic memory had been a gift of the DNA.

"Good." He pulled a small pouch from a pocket and worked out a single latex glove. "Hold out your hand. This has my prints embedded into each fingertip. You will need this to exit the facility."

"Exit the facility?"

"Still doing that, are you?"

"What?" Garik could hardly focus. This man was helping him escape? What luck! He hadn't seen this coming.

"Repeating people." He worked the glove over Garik's hand, adjusting each finger to align properly.

"Why are you doing this?"

"I need a reason?" Wilder stepped back and looked at Garik, wearing three manacles, with a chain linking one hand to his feet. "Why did you ask if I slashed my garbage bags?"

"Oh, that." Garik took a deep breath. "I read one time that agents do that to keep their trash from being stolen. It falls out if someone tries—"

"I know why I would slash my garbage bags. You said agents . . ." He paused and waited.

"Okay," Garik said, tired of the hints and

innuendos, "you have to be Mossad. It fits. You don't even have a family on Long Island, do you?"

Wilder laughed.

"Are you hybridized, too? Those arms—"

"And you have guessed entirely too much. I have never been to Long Island, but yes, I have family pictures in my wallet, and yes, they are an invention. I tell you this to get you to do something for me."

"You're helping me escape, so shoot." Garik grimaced. "Poor word choice. Sorry."

"I have secured the sword—"

"You! And they blamed me!" Garik was stunned. The whole complex emptied by Sunchaser in revenge, and this man was at fault!

"Wait! Hear me out. The technology you see around you is shared between your country and mine. The Director and Ms. Sunchaser have chosen to abuse it for personal gain. You've seen the risks they've taken, the monstrosities—"

"My friends," Garik warned, unsure where he was headed.

"People they would eliminate. People you can save, the reason I pushed for them to be transferred to the new facility."

"And the sword?"

"A distraction. Eminently vital if the technology can be made useful, but for now, only a distraction to allow you to escape."

"And do what?" He had the final page of the schematics. He knew how to "fix" the sword. He was certain Wilder didn't know that.

"That answer is difficult. However, you are capable, everything this program has worked to achieve. The Canadians will be amenable." Wilder pulled out a thin leather document holder very much like a passport. "Show this at the border, then again at the facility. You must have the sword with you."

"There's a lot unexplained, but one thing I'll need is clothes. They'll be looking for me in this."

"Excellent thought. Here." Wilder worked one minder's dart gun from the man's waist and handed it to Garik. He talked as he began to work off his uniform. "You will need to anesthetize me to make this believable. Shoot me with this gun and leave it here. Take the unused one with you. Three shots, three darts used."

"The sword?" Garik hefted the gun. It was unfamiliar to him but seemed easy to use.

"I always carry the keys to my Jeep." He was to his shorts by then, and he held out his shirt, jacket, and pants. The metal in his pocket clinked.

"Which explains nothing. Can you unlock me first?"

"Good. If they question me, I can say you begged for your freedom. I must also be able to say you were still in restraints and that I did not offer you any assistance. On the neck, please. I want the dart in my skin when they find me. You would have to remove it with the clothes anywhere else."

"Okay. Ready?"

"From behind. They must think you a coward."

Garik lifted the gun, fired, and watched the man slump to the floor. He realized he didn't know where the man's car was. A Jeep. He could find a Jeep. He rustled through the pockets, found the key to the shackles, and unlocked them.

For you, Jantzen, he thought, as he stripped and pulled on Lt. Wilder's uniform. It was snug. His socks showed, and he was forced to wear his own shoes, but it was doable. Wilder's cap fit fine. He looked at the glove on his hand, pressed Wilder's thumbprint to the passkey, and watched the display light up.

Before choosing a destination, he dragged the three men out of the elevator and tossed the two used guns after them. He kept the unused one with him as Wilder had requested.

He almost pushed the button to take him to the mall. He could picture freedom from there. Yet, Wilder would have parked in the underground garage . . . where Paul Gberie and John Carter had fallen and Jantzen had been taken from him. His stomach churned at returning to that place, but he pressed. As the door closed, he listened to the ding that said he was on his way.

— 4 —

he garage.

Close in, the parking area was separated off for the exclusive Stamford Suites in the Tower. Beyond the concrete barriers set up to keep the richies from the riffraff, blocks of parking spaces reached into the distance. Cars peppered those closer in. Even with the research center mostly emptied, some people were required to keep the facility running, and the staff in the forty-story building needed somewhere to park.

Jeep. Where was it? Jeep, Jeep, come to me, Jeep.

The key had a remote fob, and he pressed the unlock button. A beep-beep echoed in the hard-ceilinged space, and he turned, looking. Another press, and a single beep narrowed his search. He pressed it again, this time catching the flashing lights as they painted the ceiling red.

He ran that way, aware of how outside the box his actions were. Darting someone, wearing a military uniform, out and about *during a building lockdown* . . . would Rodheimer ever be angry! He grinned. He loved it. Inside the Jeep, he hit the seat adjustment button to give his long legs room, touched the starter, and checked the gauges. It was only his second time to drive a car. The first was Kevin Lee's van, and that had been a disaster. This time, no busted windows!

Approaching the exit, the gates were closed, and he considered if they would open, or if he would need to use Wilder's passkey. With the place in lockdown . . . the gates moved aside as he approached. He breathed a sigh of relief. They were set to lock people out, not keep people in.

He drove up the ramp into the sun and sat, thinking of the tracking device inside him. It was linked to whoever was assigned to monitor him. He had Wilder's passkey, likely why no one was pursuing him already. When he drove away from the building, what would happen then? He guessed he would have to drive faster, but where? All he knew was Canada and Yellowknife.

He typed in "Yellowknife" on the GPS screen, and one of the choices that pulled up was Yellowknife, Northwest Territories. Beside it, 39 hours, 2,290 miles. At least the Jeep wasn't total electric. No way would he find enough recharging stations in such a remote area.

Then the foundations for his plans began to crack. Gas cost money, and he had none. Yet, if Wilder had prepared all this, he must have made plans for that. Garik opened the console to find a thick packet of mixed bills, a valid-looking driver's license with his name and photo, and insurance on the Jeep in his name. Inside the glove box were travel documents, maps, and on one map, a red X in a red circle with no other information. Garik understood that was his destination.

Research labs. Why build only one, when the military will fund two at twice the price?

A pair of sunglasses on the dash seemed fitted just for him, and he slipped them on. He clicked Start on the navigation panel, and the image shifted, revealing the streets in Bay City, and said, "Make a right turn on Stamford Drive, then stay right to take Corona Street towards Sycamore." An arrow appeared showing his car turning right.

As the Jeep moved forward, the electric-only range showed 120 miles. The dinosaur tank was completely full. *Sorry, dinosaurs*, he thought. *You're gonna burn a second time today.* He hoped for a couple hours before he needed to suck them into the engine.

South on Sycamore took him to a left on First at the Old City Hall, past Park Avenue and the powerline right-of-way, and towards Bay City Medical and beyond to I-80 north. He was leaving his life behind, Muhammad, Ibn, Hayat, his Street Strider, his aunt, skating at the Connel Street Skate Park, his memories of Marisa, all of it. Thirty-nine hours. Could he do it?

Could he not?

Jantzen, transmorphized from Bay City to a place two thousand miles away. What had happened during that journey? A glitch in the system? A sword that Sunchaser refused to calibrate to a functional operating level because she wanted to claim the rights for her own?

How many had to suffer for the greed of people who were already rich by most people's standards?

He was just outside Bay City readying to accelerate onto the I-80 entrance ramp when a winged creature the size of a small car alighted on the roadway in front of him. He felt the Jeep slam on the brakes for him before he could react, and driver assist warnings flashed across the dash. The Jeep lurched to a stop feet before hitting the creature. Garik gulped air to calm himself before rolling down the window, leaning out, and yelling, "Justin, you idiot! I nearly hit you!"

"Yet, you didn't." The man's mantis-like jaw clacked twice when he finished speaking, a byproduct of his insect-infused bone structure giving him a jaw more suited to dismembering prey than speaking clear English.

"And, oh, my gosh, put on some clothes!" Garik leaned his head back and shut his eyes. Yet, what he had seen couldn't be unseen ever again. Eidetic. He could never forget, either visual or auditory. Curse Justin for a new memory he didn't want. The back of the Jeep opened and Justin began to rustle around.

"Did you look back here at all?" Clack, clack.

"I was running from men trying to suck out my brain. No, I didn't look back there. I saved that for you."

"How does that uniform fit?" Clack, clack.

"Why?" Garik opened his eyes and saw Justin in the rearview mirror. He had folded in on himself, put on a black knit cap pulled low over his head, and he was pushing his long, thick arms into the sleeves of a leather duster.

"Thought it might be a bit snug, you know, where it counts." The clacks were infused with humor.

"Are you making fun of me?" Garik pushed open his door and exited the Jeep. Justin was right there, nose to nose, looking as normal as a human-hybrid praying mantis can look when wearing a leather duster and knit cap. They were about the same height, and Justin began to laugh.

"Lt. Wilder's not a big guy, I gather. Nice socks." Clack, clack.

"You're still an idiot. What are you doing here?" Garik tried to pull information from his memory explaining Justin's presence *on a random highway in the middle of nowhere.*

Yet, he had pulled clothes from the back of the Jeep, and that meant he knew they would be there. If Wilder was truly Mossad—which he hadn't admitted—and the Israeli government was also in the human-hybrid game . . . had Justin been recruited for a Mossad spy?

Garik blurted, "Are you Mossad, also?"

"Psst! As American as you." The clacks continued but less noticeable.

"Hello, Mossad agent. I'm Russian." Well, Armenian, but close enough. His parents lived in Russia, and he was born there.

"Hmm." Justin looked at Garik with new respect. "You've grown a bite with your new height. Ron told me to expect it—"

"Ron?" Repeating information, but Garik didn't care.

"Lt. Wilder. Get with me, my friend." Justin bumped a pincher-like hand against Garik's forehead. "You have clothes in the back that will fit. We need to find a rest stop—"

"I can change here." Wilder's uniform was indeed cutting off circulation, and Justin's reminder was making the tight fit more and more uncomfortable.

"But." Justin paused for effect. "I. Can't. Remove. Your. Tracking. Device. Here."

"Thank you." Relief flooded Garik. "I was worried about that."

"So are we. Rodheimer and Brace have to think you've disappeared, not that you're heading to Yellowknife. Get in. You can drive or I can."

"My driver's license and insurance. You ride shotgun."

"Fine with me."

As Justin turned, Garik noted how the wings fit nicely into the broad shoulders cut into the coat. Almost as if he were totally, completely, one-hundred-percent human.

Something neither of them could claim.

JUSTIN MADE sure Garik carried Lt. Wilder's passkey in with them. In a stall, he ran a scanning device over Garik, finally asking him to remove his shirt. The device beeped repeatedly at his lower back, just where Garik wouldn't be able to reach it easily if he wanted to remove the tracking beacon himself.

"Can't I just keep Wilder's passkey in my pocket?" Garik didn't like the size of the knife Justin held in his hand.

"When he is found and they can't locate his passkey, they will disengage it. They will begin searching for your beacon, and you are sending out to half of

North America. It has to be out and now."

"Okay, but—" and Garik lurched as the knife buried into his back. "Yi-yi-yi, please finish!"

"When I find it." After another thirty seconds, Justin proclaimed, "Got it!"

"Let me see." Garik straightened. He placed his hand on the wound, only to feel smooth skin, the damage from the tracker already healed. The pain was with him forever, however. That's what eidetic meant . . . he never forgot.

A small device, a chip, likely, with a glowing red light and a tiny antenna. It and four inches of the knife's blade were stained red.

"Can I smash it?" Garik took his new shirt from a pile, worked his arms into the sleeves, and pulled it over his head. He dropped Wilder's pants and kicked them aside.

"Got something better." Justin handed him a worn pair of jeans. "These, and I have cloth boaters for you in the sack. We're changing your look."

"I like my look." Garik grinned as he slipped the jeans on. They buttoned at his waist, a perfect fit. "What are you doing with that?"

"I'm sending you south, hopefully as far as Mexico."

"How?" Garik was pretty sure Yellowknife and Canada were a long way to the north.

"A military-grade drone in the car. We're attaching

this and Ron's passkey to it and sending it off. Where it crashes, no one knows."

"At least we won't. I'm sure the Director will."

"Distraction. Diversion." Justin gave him a clumsy thumbs up with his pincher-like hands. "And before you ask, you were right about Ron. And Mossad has made his Jeep as invisible as possible, so that should give us some protection. It's why we don't have watches or any other mobile devices with us." Justin had bagged the uniform, and he handed it to Garik.

"Except for the car's GPS." Garik had his shoes on and noted the worn look, like they had been his favorites for months. He approved.

"It runs on a virtual private network. It pings Europe if anyone's looking."

"Cool." One of his aunt's words. Irina had always liked old-fashioned terms. Using it reminded him of her. Good times that he could never bring back again.

"Ready?" Justin put his hand on the door latch.

Garik nodded, and they stepped out together into a stream of leather-covered, tattoo-inked bikers entering. The lead man, as tall as Garik and Justin, with a long beard and shoulders like a bear, took them in and nodded.

"My apologies for interrupting. No discrimination here. What you do on your time is your business." The others with him nodded their agreement.

"Thank you. I appreciate your open-minded attitude." Garik grinned, and he tugged Justin out the door.

"What?" Justin looked back to the restrooms, and he had a shocked expression. "Did he think . . . that we . . . how dare he!"

"It's funny. Laugh about it." Garik slapped him in the chest with the back of his hand. "Where's that drone? I want my tracking device in Mexico."

They found it in the back of the Jeep next to the electrified sword.

"Wilder said I had to have this. He didn't tell me where it was. He can truthfully say he told me nothing and didn't offer me any help. I hope he makes it okay."

"You darted him, right?" Justin was setting up the drone. It had a built-in tray for the passkey and the tracking device.

"Pow, pow, you're dead."

Justin looked at him hard.

"Well, anesthetized." Garik shrugged.

Justin's expression relaxed, and he started up the drone. It lifted and sped away towards the south. He set the control back into the car, told Garik he was driving, and they were off to Canada . . . by way of Nevada, Idaho, Montana, and every place in between.

$-5-$

arik opened his eyes to the glow of dash lights on Justin Kurtew's beak-like jaw. He still wore the knit cap and duster. His wrists extended from the sleeves, thickened, a Popeye caricature, and his hands seemed more pincers than fingers.

What was normal? How much could a man change and still remain who he was? Devon Maye's story of before and after, about his mother as an Olympic hopeful, to have her hopes dashed with a medical diagnosis that said she might not live to see her son married . . .

yet, to Devon, she was the same person, someone who loved him more than life itself. Before and after, no difference.

Garik hadn't known Justin truly *before*, but he had seen the man make dramatic changes. He had been a man before, mostly, and now? Mantis almost completely. Yet, the bantering personality, the person that was static electricity in every conversation, the in-your-face response to things he didn't agree with hadn't changed. Justin was still Justin.

Garik wasn't sure he could say the same about himself. How far would his "after" take him? Was he there yet?

"You're awake." A single clack, subtle, as though Justin was trying to control it.

"Where are we?" Garik's voice was thick, and he cleared his throat, more of a rumble than a ripple.

"Idaho. Not much here, so I can't say much more. I just follow the little arrow on the screen. Did you growl at me?"

"I don't think so." Garik adjusted his position to relieve pressure on his back. His voice still felt thick. "Where you stabbed me is uncomfortable."

"I enjoyed that, by the way. Even-stevens for what you did to me in the ring."

"I'll do worse if you stab me again. Find somewhere to stop. I need to get out and stretch."

"Rest stop in thirty-seven miles. Are you good that

long?"

"Sure." He reached behind the seat and rustled through several bags. They had stocked up for the road at a convenience store with a small ice chest, prepackaged meats, and other snackeries. A bag of chips rustled, and he pulled it into the front seat with him.

"Cheddar or vinegar?"

"Let me look." Garik held it up, read aloud, "Salt-and-vinegar," and popped the top of the bag to release a crisp, pungent aroma.

"Strong." Justin didn't indicate approval or disapproval, just a fact.

"You were with Joanie in the city. What happened?" The third person in Justin's group was last seen face down in the garage looking pretty dead.

"Like are we alive? Some of us." He clacked, less subtly, revealing emotion. "Giselle, Julia, and Paolo—"

"With Jantzen, I know." The memory haunted him.

"Your eyeshine really shows up at night. I've got the dash lights down, can barely see you, and you read that chip wrapper like it's daylight."

"Yeah." Glad to be distracted, he put a chip in his mouth and sat up, nearly spitting it out. He chewed it, cardboard, and swallowed with difficulty.

"What?"

"Who could eat this?" He held up the bag and looked for the expiration date, certain they had gone stale LIKE LAST YEAR.

"You picked them. Let me taste."

Garik held out the open bag, Justin groped for it, as though he couldn't find it in the dark, then worked out a chip. He crunched it, pronounced it stringently acidic, and said they tasted like normal vinegar-and-salt to him.

"I can't eat them. Do you want any?"

"Like I said, you picked them."

"Okay." Garik rolled the top, leaned over the seat, returned them to the sack, and dug in the ice chest for a package of bratwurst. He bit into one, and the flavor rolled down his throat like a sultry night in the desert, warm, comforting, and no distractions.

"Have you noticed that's all you're eating?"

"Not especially." Yet, he had. None of the grain-based snacks had appealed to him, but none had put him off like the chips. Yeah, Justin, he had noticed. "Let me know when we reach the rest stop."

"Like a bullhorn."

"Idiot." Garik laid his head against the door and let the motion of the car lull him into darkness.

THE REST stop was like daylight.

To Garik, anyway. As they pulled in, he came awake and tried to sit up. The Jeep rocked as Justin pulled over a speed hump, and Garik released a ragged breath.

"Sorry, man. I didn't pick the car."

"My back. I don't know why I hurt. I never have before."

"Lucky you." Justin pulled into a spot, killed the dinosaur engine, and said, "Bullhorn."

"I used to hate you." Garik worked his feet into his shoes.

"And I spoiled that how?"

"You haven't. I hurt too much to care right now."

"Baby. Take a walk."

"On the wild side?" Garik chuckled. He released the door, and the interior of the Jeep was like a strobe. He closed his eyes to let them adjust.

"To look at you, yeah. I didn't bring a shaving kit."

"It's a man's world. Preparing for Canada." Garik pulled himself from the car. "Don't leave without me."

He put his hand on his back where the knife had removed the tracker and realized that was only a small amount of it. Every part of him felt different, out of sorts, like when he was thirteen and growing, hurting all the time. He looked to the building, saw the men's sign, and stepped inside. In the mirror, he saw what Justin had seen. He was alone and stripped off his shirt, breathed in deeply, anger looking back at him in the image.

Wolf boy. Werewolf. Sideshow act. He looked at his fingers, searching for Christian's wolfhound hands. His nails, coarser, perhaps, but not claws, not yet.

"What have you people done to me?" he asked the

mirror, balling his hand. He hardly recognized his voice, didn't want more changes, and smashed his fist into the glass, only to discover it wasn't glass but polished stainless steel. The metal deformed, dimpled the concrete block behind it, and held. Garik pulled his hand back, his throat giving off a whimpering sound that turned into a growl.

"Same old story." Justin stood at the door. "Don't mean to intrude, but this is the only restroom, and even us weirdos can't go in the open. Sorry. The highway department won't be happy about that mirror."

"You see me? Look at me."

"I'm not blind, just weird." Justin held up his hand and pretended to study it. "Yeah, still weird."

"Does it ever stop?" The changes, the distance between where he began and where he ended. The before and after. The losing everything he once treasured as important and having a future so unfamiliar he couldn't fathom it.

"Do you see me?" Justin snorted. "I *molt.* There is no stopping, not until what Corona Corporation has done to us runs its course."

"I'm supposed to be their super soldier."

"So was I. Welcome to reality. Since you're here, hold my coat." He began pulling off his duster.

"Nah, Justin!" Garik turned his head. He'd seen enough of the man on the road.

"Now who's the idiot? I have on clothes under this.

What'd you used to say? Sheesh!" He tossed the duster to Garik and entered the stall.

Garik stepped outside. He didn't know what sounds mantises made when doing their business, and he didn't think he wanted to find out.

GARIK WAS surprised when they crossed into Canada. The border guards looked at his passport from Lt. Wilder, took a similar one from Justin, made some phone calls, noted the plates on the Jeep, and passed them through.

"How did that happen?" Garik had fully planned to skirt the checkpoint and had assumed that was the reason for the Jeep. Go anywhere through any terrain, then back on the road again.

"Mossad. There's mutual support between the countries." Justin brushed it off.

"Nah, this is about the program. After they called in, they never looked at you twice, and you're something to look at."

"Said the wolf with the big eyes to Little Red Riding Hood."

"Sheesh. Let me know when you want me to drive." Garik leaned his seat back. Now his legs hurt. What was going on with them?

There was no sleep to be found, and he watched the countryside evaporate behind them, in places revealing glinting patches of winter snow. He tried to see Jantzen but couldn't picture him without the purple mist. Would Jantzen know him? Or would he have changed so much that he would be just another Justin, a cast-off, a true cipher in the boundless Yellowknife wilderness?

THIRTY-NINE hours had turned into nearly forty-eight, with refueling stops, the border crossing, and Garik's increasing need to get out of the Jeep, move around, as Justin called it, pacing like a wolf, taking in the Canadian aromas, sniffing the air, learning of the new world around him. It was his first time this far north, wild country compared to Bay City, and he wanted to be out in it.

Not crammed into a Jeep that was feeling smaller by the mile.

By the time they reached Hwy 3—the Yellowknife Highway around Great Slave Lake—wood bison shared their journey, looking up as they passed, then ignoring the disruption and returning to grazing. A mile of steel girder bridge leapfrogged the Mackenzie River as they drove past lake after lake after lake.

After a night in Yellowknife, they headed out on Ingraham Trail, marked as Hwy 4, the reason for the Jeep, as Garik quickly realized. The pavement ran out less than an hour along the road, and then that turned to gravel. The red X on his map seemed truly to be in the middle of nowhere. The road ended at Tibbitt Lake, but a track cut off before then, the only possible path to the

Canadian facility.

"They wanted to get away from it all, didn't they?" Garik was driving, and he navigated the Jeep like he stole it, often in 4-wheel low, gunning the engine over rutted sections, and working through snowmelt that seemed determined to swallow the tires for an afternoon snack.

"Just keep driving." Justin wasn't in a better mood. The trip had become a slog, from the sunny West Coast to the remains of a winter not long over. Coats were becoming necessary, and only Justin had one of those.

They topped a rise to find a stone and dirt embankment blocking their way. WARNING, a sign said. Underneath, written in smaller letters, GOVERNMENT FACILITY – NO ENTRANCE PERMITTED.

"This must be it." Garik searched for a gate, guards maybe, to whom they could show their identification and get inside.

"Seems so. I'll be right back." Justin opened the door, walked to the back of the Jeep, and rooted around. He returned with earbuds and a watch, which he was strapping to his thick wrist. The strap was especially long, meaning it was designed just for him.

"You had a watch." Meaning, *you had a phone.* "And you couldn't tell me."

"No, I couldn't," Justin said, and he tapped on the phone's face, waking it, and tapped again. He spoke, "We're here." After a moment, he spoke again, less polite. "Who do you think is driving for two days to get here and parked outside the gate? And yes, he has it. Open up, you fruitcake."

"Fruitcake?" Garik found reason to be amused.

"Ron set this up. They've surveilled us the past two hours. This is a Mossad-supplied vehicle with all the signatures that should provide them, and I'm tired. No offense, wolf boy, but the dog smell is about to get to me."

Dog smell. Something Garik hadn't noticed. What else had he missed? A section of the stone wall in front of them dropped into the ground, and Justin waved Garik ahead, telling him it was the point of the Jeep. Drive over the embankment. The other side revealed nothing except more trees, grass, and mounds of rotting snow.

"Now?" Garik watched behind them as the stone wall filled the gap once again.

"Go. Look for the red flare. It takes us underground."

Again. Garik was tired of being underground. Did no one like living in the sun? Sheesh! He pulled forward, finally locating the flare burning half a mile ahead.

— 6 —

arik slammed the Jeep to a stop, called out, "I can't," and the world around him shifted to a kaleidoscopic rainbow of colors.

They were at the entrance to the underground complex. Justin sitting next to him froze, a rainbow man dressed in surprise. The trees in the landscape, poplar, spruce, pine, birch, and fir leapfrogged in fantastic rainbows to grasp the pristine Canadian sky. A man just ahead held a flare. He was stepping their way, forever with one foot in the air, ready to tread on the sturdy buffalo grass and sheep fescue that littered the walled-in compound.

Garik threw the door back, sending a wave of rainbows rippling through the air. He was beside the Jeep, then twenty feet away, then forty, breathing deep, taking in the forest aroma of poplar and pine and fir. It was if he had never lived, as if he needed this just to be alive. To drive below ground? It was an impossible request. Who could live in such a place? He would be crushed, his soul imprisoned, his spirit silenced forever.

He counted off without realizing he was doing so, sixteen, seventeen, eighteen . . . what was his life worth? How much did he have to pay to exact revenge for what had been done to him? Twenty-two, twenty-three . . . Mama, Papa . . . twenty-four . . . Jantzen, you abandoned me . . . twenty-five, twenty-six . . . his time was about up, and he released the rainbows, watched them evaporate into the clear Canadian sky, the wisps of their passing a longing he could never fulfill.

It was what he wanted to do, evaporate into the world around him, enter nature, never return. It called to him, the wilderness. He'd sensed it on the drive up, stronger and stronger, hadn't known what it was. Now he knew. This was where he was meant to be.

And no, not in the underground facility they'd driven forty-eight hours to reach. The wilderness, the wide-open landscape that ran as far as he could see, smell, hear, and taste.

Freedom. He'd always craved it. Now, there it was, just on the other side of the wall, even now being taken from him once again.

"HEY, GARIK, man, what was that?"

Garik turned to see Justin. He had pulled himself over the driver's seat and leaned halfway out of the door. In front of the Jeep, the man with the flare had dropped it and was raising his gun. Garik let the rainbows flare. Four seconds. That was what he had, plenty of time. In rainbow waves, the air moved out of his way, and he had the gun in his hand. He removed the ammunition and threw it far, far past the wall before returning the gun to the man's holster. Thirty, and he let the rainbows go once more, this time in the first ragged throes of pending exhaustion.

Thirty seconds. That's all he got before he had to recharge. Not worth much, was it, for a super soldier, the best of the best?

"Stop that, Garik!" This time, Justin made it all the way out of the Jeep. He called to the man with the gun, "Don't shoot—"

He already had the weapon located, had drawn it again, and with Garik suddenly at arm's length, he aimed the gun and pulled the trigger. The lack of a report surprised him, and he tried to fire again.

"You have no ammunition," Garik said, leaning over to rest his hands on his upper legs. "Justin, tell him

I don't intend to get shot. Had that done, not fun."

Justin arrived about that time, took the gun from the man, and threw it to the side where it landed in the grass. A siren now wailed from underground.

"He could have kept the gun." Garik stood, feeling some of his energy returning. He looked at the man's name on his shirt. Williams.

"Not and shoot you."

"He had no ammunition. I removed it."

"No way," Williams said. "No effin' way!"

Several other men with weapons came running up the ramp, and they held their rifles while Williams retrieved his pistol and checked the ammunition.

"The entire magazine's gone. Where—"

"Over the wall," Garik said. "Where I want to be."

"Impossible," Williams insisted. "You didn't have time—"

"That's why your brass has worked so hard to get this man here. His DNA magic allows him to *make* the time." Justin asked Garik, "What do you need?"

"Food. Someplace to sit."

A man came striding out, and the soldiers holding the weapons made room for him. At a motion of his hand, they dropped their guns. He walked directly to Justin.

"Major Kevin Linkletter. You must be Justin. I'm glad to meet you. Did Lt. Wilder secure everything you needed?"

"We're here. Your man made us nearly dead." He nodded at Williams.

"Williams?" Linkletter's voice hardened. "Can you explain?"

"They were on their way in, sir, just as we expected. All they had to do was drive down the ramp. The hairy one got out of the vehicle . . . I take that back, Major. He didn't even get out. He was suddenly there, and there. He didn't move, just reappeared. I raised my weapon per procedure, and then he was in front of me. He did something with my pistol. I drew again and fired, only my magazine is somewhere beyond the perimeter."

"Explain *drew again*, soldier."

"I was lifting my pistol, and then it was back in my holster—"

Garik began to retch. He doubled over, held to Justin's arm, and fell to one knee.

"Food?" Justin knelt beside him.

"Yes. Doing that takes it out of me." It was worse than before, though. He was changing again. The soldier had summed it up. The hairy one. He might as well have said the werewolf. Garik felt the difference. The call of the wild. The need to be there and not here.

"This is the man Rodheimer and Sunchaser planned to cull?" Linkletter asked Justin.

"Crude, Major, but yes. Can we get him inside?"

"Inside," Garik managed to get out. He started to

refuse, but the grass on the ground blurred, and he did a faceplant before he could say no.

"BACK UNDERGROUND again." Garik didn't need to open his eyes. He could smell it, the antiseptic cleanness of it all, unlike the Corona Tower facility, which prided itself on smelling like nothing at all. In addition, a whiff of brown soil, dead leaves, growing things, someone he knew. "Justin?"

"And someone else you want to see. Open your eyes, pretty boy."

"Snarky as always." Garik peeled his eyelids back as he drew himself up. A yawn overtook him, and he arched his back and stretched.

Like a dog would do.

He caught it, tried to stop it, instead drew in a deep breath through his nose, dissecting each portion of each aroma that assaulted him. Justin's mantis. His own, fur and dander, the rub of a hand against a favorite pet. A deep-sea saltiness, a touch of the shore, an ocean breeze.

"Jantzen?" It had to be.

"Almost. Don't expect too much." Justin called, "Jantz, come meet Garik."

Come meet? That was ominous. They already knew one another. He wanted to ask Justin to explain, then a trim man with a black beard and eyes with a purple tint walked into the room, held out a hand as if to shake and said, "Garik. Hello. I understand we know one another."

"Yes." Garik took the hand. The skin, familiar but different. The teasing, the challenges the man liked to dunk him in, the forcing him to be more than he wanted to be, smarter, quicker, more attentive. That's what was missing.

"We worked together in the States at the other facility. Am I right?" He glanced at Justin as if making sure he had his information correct.

"Yes. You were my teacher." And friend and co-conspirator and anchor when my life was falling apart.

"Ah, then not together. Not as equals. Interesting. Perhaps—" Jantzen stopped, his expression frozen, and his eyes . . . this was what Tim-o had described to him. Jantzen's eyes blazed purple before fading, and he picked up where he left off. "—we will meet again. We can discuss it in more depth."

He was met by a woman who took his elbow and said, "This way, Dr. Hefferly. Dinner is waiting. You don't want to miss dinner, do you?"

"What happened?" Garik at least knew now why Jantzen hadn't returned to let him know he was alive. Because he wasn't, not really.

"They're not even sure why he's here. The sword shouldn't have worked at all. Yet somehow it did. Halfway, as you can see, but there's that."

"Yeah, there's that. Is outside time possible around

here?"

"Want to see a mirror first? And the team here wants to check you out physically."

"You've got to be kidding me." Garik felt his lips pull into a snarl. "I've been checked to the core. They know everything there is to know about me."

"Maybe not. They tell me there's evidence that injury can jumpstart new DNA-induced transformations. Remember that tracker we took out?"

"The knife you stabbed in my back?"

"Yes, sorry." Justin didn't seem very sorry. "It looks like we have a good reason not to get injured. All the fights I got into? That's likely the reason my body has gone extreme."

"Should'a been a better person, huh?"

"Likely. Now, up from there. We've got someplace we need to be."

Garik tossed the blanket back, saw he was still fully clothed, and checked his arms for any attachments and found only two bandages.

"Already gone. Once you got filled up, I told them to take the bags away."

"Thank you, I guess." He tested sitting up, found it felt fine, and rose to his feet. "Outside's not a thing then."

"It can be, just not now. You know they've got a runway here. Not many people drive in like we did. Anyway, people do get outside, part of the reason for putting this facility here. Less chance for observation by the nosy neighbors."

"Quit trying to distract me. Why do I need to see a mirror?"

"You did notice your arms?"

"Somewhat." At the rest stop. Just now. And trying to ignore them.

"Sure then, let's do this cold turkey and hope people recognize you. Follow me." Justin led the way out of the room.

One thing Garik just realized. Justin wasn't in his duster. Shirt. Pants. And when he turned to exit the room, his neatly tucked wings were available for everyone to see.

What sort of place was this? Oh, right, Canada, where everyone accepts everyone else for exactly who they are, and no one steps on anyone's toes ever.

"KIDDO!" A tall, Nordic-featured man was the first to see Garik, and he ran to the door to greet him.

"Devo, how are you here?" Garik had pictured the move from the West Coast as a forced event for the hybrids alone. Devon, the activities director at the Corona Tower research center, was as un-hybrid as they came.

"Heard you might be joining us. How could I resist?"

"Heard from whom?" For two weeks, Garik had

been stuck on the fortieth floor of Corona Tower with no information about what was happening in the basement facility that served as the research center for the human-hybrid project. Then he was given the terminal news that they intended to suck his brains to share it with three hundred volunteers who wanted to become him.

When did people plan to begin telling *him* something?

"Let's say word gets around."

"Wilder, right? I know he's Mossad."

"Kiddo, I knew you'd figure it out. Course, I didn't know any of it. No one tells me stuff. I'm just the hired hand. But, this is Canada! I've always wanted to come here!"

"Skiing, right?" Garik remembered the snow.

"For my mom. Now, let's get you to the party. You might know a few people."

And he did. Stephen to Veronika to Jacquelien and all the way to Raphaël, Joachim, and Melanie.

"Where's the twins?" He couldn't find them. They were like walking sore thumbs getting on everyone's nerves. They must be around.

"Yah, here!" In walked Andrey and Anatoli Burgorski carrying two kegs. "Anyone here under nineteen?"

"Sorry, kiddo," Devon said. "It's a joke on you."

Garik played along. A hybrid's body couldn't get high. For the rest of the party, the joke was on them.

— 7 —

here's a real chance this will work." Garik couldn't see how they could be so *dense*, so *hard-headed*, so unwilling to try something so *obvious.*

"We have only your word you can do this, and that's not enough." Dee Thomas, the senior outside project liaison, stood against an outsize monitor filling the wall. To the back of the room sat Major Linkletter, his legs crossed in a casual manner, alongside Shervaughnna Honda, assistant project scientist; Andrea Ho, assistant researcher; and Lauren Irons, assistant specialist for the AMS lab, or as Garik had learned, the American Mutant Services lab.

The screen showed the back of the Jeep, open with a bar of sky across the top and the bumper and part of a clump of buffalo grass below. Inside, the empty drone case. Next to it, the sword, surrounded by cloth, bunched where the sword had been unwrapped enough to identify it as real and present.

The Jeep was now parked underground with the sword being studied in an alternate location.

"You've already said you don't know what's wrong. I do. I can fix it." Garik was out of patience with these people. Sure, Canada, acceptance, and all that; and they had made room for his friends from the Corona Tower facility. Yet, his frustration mounted by the moment. Did he have to bash their heads to get them to understand? This concerned Jantzen, part of his pack. How could he not try anything to make sure this happened to no one else?

"James, will you please help Mr. Shayk understand how this works?" Thomas nodded to James Ku, a bland-faced man with an easy expression and dark, lifeless hair. He wore a white jacket with Ku stitched onto the pocket and sat with everyone else around a U-shaped table.

"Yes, please. Thank you, Dee." He lifted a remote from the table and aimed it at the screen. The image changed to show a badly cropped photograph with several large machines, some with glowing lights, and an open area surrounded by a framework of bulky projector-style *things*. Ku indicated with a laser pointer as he spoke. "This is the receiving bay for incoming transmissions. In *theory* we can dematerialize any object and transport it any distance. It does require line of sight. It isn't magic."

"Satellites, sure. You say *in theory*. So, it doesn't work." Garik felt his frustration building. Plain, people. Quit with the half meanings. These are people we are talking about.

"Oh, yes." Ku's voice brightened with excitement. "It works well. Inanimate objects, we've done plenty of those. Successfully, though not over thousands of miles. That was the California end of the project. We've yet to understand why a *sword* was chosen. The transfer device could be designed in any shape."

"So *this* doesn't work." Garik stood, wrenched the remote from Ku's hand, and shifted the image to the sword in the back of the Jeep. "Yet, it got a man here. I saw the electricity from the end of the sword dismember him molecule by molecule."

"That's what makes this exciting—" Ku vibrated with enthusiasm.

"Exciting!" Garik slammed his hand on the table, leaving a dinner plate size impression.

"Mr. Shayk, if you will." Thomas held out her hand for the remote.

"Tell me about this." Garik walked to the screen, pressed the side of his fist against the picture of the sword, and held it there. "No theories, no explanations why it won't work. It got Jantzen Hefferly here. You've admitted that—"

"We've yet to confirm anything. He is here, yes. Why, we are unsure. The remote, please." Thomas still held out her hand.

"Here's what *I* can confirm. Sunchaser never completed the sword. She intentionally left it unfinished. To kill people? I can't say, but to retain the technology for herself, that's obvious."

"And yet you have no proof."

"Proof?" Garik heard the thickness in his voice, his anger reducing his words to a near growl, his eyes making the scene before him red around the edges. "There's a layer of schematics she never released. Let me have access to it—"

"The danger is unacceptable. We've yet to understand why it does not work properly—"

"*I* understand. Can't I get you to see that? This doesn't have to happen to anyone else." His words cracked. "And maybe it could help Jantzen . . ."

"We are uncertain how this could help him. There are rules we must follow—"

Garik cut off Dee Thomas, growling, "Then I must make my own rules," and he handed her the remote, now crushed against his fist of anger. When he reached the door, locked as always, he didn't hesitate. He twisted the handle until the stressed metal snapped in his hand, leaving a torn spot in the door and exposing the interior mechanism. Garik forced the metal back until he could reach his hand inside, pulled at the locking mechanism until it groaned and snapped. He threw the door wide and turned into the corridor with a sinewy grace that became a loping run the direction where he knew the sword was.

His hand? He had left blood behind, but it was healed before he was gone ten steps. It would take longer for his timber wolf DNA to initiate his next level of changes, but he could deal with that.

Someone had to do something, their rules or his. Even the sirens and blinking lights didn't slow him down.

"TRY TO stop me." Garik twisted his neck, lifted his head, and felt the changes in his jawline. Ripping through the door was already coming home. A growl, this time from within his chest, a new sound.

"The instrument is under study, Mr. Shayk." Aldo Ku, lookalike twin to James Ku from earlier, specialist in DNA mapping and sequencing, blocked his way into the research lab hiding the sword.

"My name is Garik. If you don't like that, your other option is Wolfman. Got it? I am going in."

Ku sighed. "You're the one from the West Coast,

right?" He studied Garik's face. "My brother said . . . I didn't recognize you. The pictures were more, um—"

"Human?" The word was an angry slash. He caught *one*. Not man, not volunteer. Not person. Garik was none of those anymore.

"No, that's not what I meant. I expected a teenager."

"I'm what you got, thanks to timber wolf DNA that I didn't want and can't get rid of. I can take the door off the hinges if you need me to."

"So we know. Can I at least call someone?"

"Will they try to stop me?" The sirens and emergency lights still flashed along the corridors. No guns had shown up yet. Likely the Canadians were told to smile first and shoot later.

"Let me call. Maybe I can get the sirens silenced."

Please, Garik, thought. The high-pitched wail had his patience shattered, and he was afraid of what he might do if these people forced his hand. He stepped into the room, waited beside a desk while Ku lifted a corded phone and made a call. Across the room, the sword lay on a table with various tools around it. Thick power cables snaked across the floor, and two people, a man and a woman, studied schematic diagrams on a wall screen. They shuffled through a stack of paper, and occasionally they adjusted the image, compared the paper to the image, enlarged a section, only to make notes on the paper and go to another page.

Ku hung up the phone, and Garik noticed the sirens were gone.

"Thank you."

"I haven't told you the results of my conversation yet."

"Okay, then for the sirens." He didn't tell him he had overheard every word. He already knew they would allow him to "show" the missing schematic page "if he could." They wanted to demonstrate good faith before they kicked him out the door.

As if they had the power, he thought.

"We have fifty-nine schematic pages. The device was completed by Halo Sunchaser. None of us here worked on it, so we have to trust her—"

"Don't." Garik's chest rumbled at the thought of how the woman had lied to him over and over.

"Don't trust her? She is highly respected and very brilliant."

"And with a grandmother in South Africa suffering a blood disorder. She will do anything . . ." and the gears in Garik's head began to click and turn and give him a possible answer. "She never intended to sell the technology for the sword."

"How's that? The technology, when successfully tested, will be priceless on the world stage. When we learned she was keeping its advanced stage of completion from us, we all assumed—"

"Her grandmother. She intended to modify it as a

device to heal her grandmother. It must be. She's already wealthy. The money can't be the driving force behind doing something so foolhardy. She had to know she would be found out. There must have been a personal motivation."

"It could be possible. The mechanism is designed to reassemble transported items in optimal condition."

"You've sent damaged things through to see?"

"No." Ku was walking Garik toward the sword and the two people working on the schematics. "There was no reason to. We were looking to see that items sent through did not suffer damage, not that the machine would repair it."

"Then let me show you what I know, things I suspect you haven't even thought of yet."

"Big words, Mr., um, Garik." Ku turned and introduced him to the other two people. "Damon Lonon, molecular biologist. He keeps your liver from winding up in your head. Jennifer Landa is our forensic pathologist. When your liver winds up in your head, she helps to tell us why. Damon, Jennifer, Garik says there's another page of schematics we haven't seen yet. We're hoping he can produce it for us."

Damon looked at Garik, and he grinned. "My grandfather used to listen to a Texas radio announcer named Wolfman Jack. Any relation?"

"Was he big and hairy?"

"Ah, man, you would ask that. A beard, maybe. He

died a long time ago."

"I don't guess we'll ever find out."

Jennifer offered Garik a tablet and a stylus, saying, "A missing schematic page. Okay, then. Draw what you know."

"Do you have a pen and paper?"

Damon laughed. "Pen and paper? What? Were you raised by wolves?"

Garik smiled. It looked that way, didn't it? He decided Damon might be alright, for a mostly human guy who might one day keep his liver from winding up in his head.

Aldo Ku came up with the paper Garik requested, and of course they had pens. Garik looked through the papers with the schematics, and he sorted them out on a wide table, pointing out various parts and explaining what they did. From time to time, Jennifer said, "Oh, I see." Damon occasionally let out, "Hot dog!" Aldo Ku watched, took notes, and occasionally whispered into a black-faced smart watch on his wrist.

Eventually, Jennifer asked, "What about the schematic we don't have? I can see something's missing here," and she touched one page and sent it to the large monitor, "but what?"

"That's key, to first see what's missing. That's what I'm about to give you."

Garik began to draw, quickly, accurately, and with no hesitation. Eidetic. Photographic. He transferred the image in his head to the paper, easy as that. A printer he could plug into his brain would be quicker, but that's what his hands were for, that was, as long as they remained hands and not paws.

Christian Maguire flashed through his mind, a man who had been in Bay City, then here, and who had moved on before Garik got to see him, likely to Israel to participate in their human-hybrid program. Christian had been haunted by his wolfhound DNA, becoming more hound than human at the end, an archetype of what Garik might one day become. He shook it off. Worry didn't improve the future. Action did, and that's what he was doing, whatever it took to ensure the best outcome for his current endeavor.

Jennifer's eyes opened wide as the missing schematic reached completion. She touched one part, said, "Yes, I see," and seemed to be engrossed.

Damon kept grinning, unable to wipe his excitement off his face.

Aldo Ku was back on the phone. He said into the receiver, "Major, I think we have something here."

Garik thought, *Of course you do. What do you think I am, only human? I'm better than that, any day of the week.* Weekends? That was yet to be decided.

For you, Jantzen, he thought, as Damon clapped him on the back in excitement. *If this helps anyone, I hope it helps you.*

— 8 —

hat do you mean the sword has nothing to do with me? I'm the one who brought it to you. Have you forgotten that little detail?" Garik was livid, and after giving them the final page of schematics to finally bring it to working completion.

"And you have received sanctuary as promised to the Israeli government. And our gratitude, of course. This will mean a vast leg up to the Canadian program, and of course those countries we are aligned with." Major Linkletter sat behind a green, military-issue desk.

The top was as cleared as the man was direct. One folder sat off to the side, and it was closed, the same as the man's mind.

"Do your people even understand it?" Garik did, inside and out. He could picture each page of the schematics in his head, overlay each on the previous one, and *feel* how it should work. Jennifer and Damon had been struggling just to understand the concepts until he had begun to explain.

"You seem to be misguided, Mr. Shayk. My people are not the ones with a lack of understanding. They are highly trained and the best in their fields. The device is an intricate piece of machinery, and it will take time to work out how your information fits into the whole, but we will do it." Linkletter stood, dismissing Garik, and he turned to a file cabinet at the side of the room and opened a drawer, thumbing through but not selecting anything to pull out.

Corporal Rory Williams, the man whose pistol Garik had disabled, stood from the chair at his side and motioned for Garik to also rise. Cpl. Williams wasn't a small man, but Garik felt outsized next to him. Garik had filed a protest when he was excluded from the laboratory working on the sword, and Williams had been his guide to meet with Linkletter. He wore a green patterned operational uniform with a khaki cap and black boots.

Once away from Linkletter's office, Garik offered a

peace branch. "I like the uniform."

Williams cut him off sharply. "No, you cannot wear one. You are no longer in the States."

"Did I ask to? Sheesh. I was being nice. Are you still angry about the pistol?"

"The pistol." Williams stopped and turned to study Garik's face. "You embarrassed me in front of the Major, and you ask if I'm still angry. What do you think?"

"And I was supposed to let you shoot me?"

"You were supposed to drive down the ramp, not get out of the Jeep and do whatever it was you did. That's what you were supposed to do."

Another soldier, a woman, rounded a corner and walked toward them. Williams drew up, nodded as she passed, said, "Ma'am," and waited until she was out of sight.

"Fine," Garik said. He held out his arms with his wrists butted together. "Throw me in the brig. Then you can feel better about yourself."

Williams looked at him for a few moments, then shook his head and continued down the corridor.

"Wait, Corporal, or Williams, or whatever I should call you. You haven't handcuffed me yet. Let me pay my dues. I've been a bad boy, and I want to be your friend. Please?" Garik chased after him, dancing around him, while he continued to offer his wrists.

"Stop, please." Williams narrowed his eyes at him,

then motioned for him to follow, and he opened a door, and they stepped inside. He closed the door.

"No lock," Garik said. He tried the door, it opened back up, and he latched it again. He did it once more before being satisfied.

"Are you teasing me?" Williams began to puff up.

"Seriously, no lock. In Bay City, every door was locked, and we had to have a passkey to move anywhere."

"We have locks here. Plenty of them." He pulled a lanyard from his shirtfront with a keycard on it then dropped it back inside.

"That door is not locked." Garik nodded his head its direction. "Enough of that. Why are we in here?"

"They kidnapped you when you were in high school?" Williams took on an expression of amazement.

Garik sighed. "It was the summer before my senior year, but yes. I found my way into the research center, and they refused to let me out."

"So, did you choose your wolf thing . . . or?"

Garik laughed.

"I've seen some of the others. Yours is the one I'd want, that is if that was something I ever wanted to do, which it isn't."

"I was knocked out, and when I woke up . . ." Garik shrugged. "Well, I woke up, and they said, 'Sorry, guy, you aren't you any longer,' and now I'm me."

"Man," Williams said with a whistle. "Sometime can you meet with a few of us? We've seen the people coming from there, and we've all got questions."

"The Major will let you?" Garik thought of Colonel Brace in Bay City. He'd slice some stuff off rather than be nice to people.

"He's a bit gruff but not a bad boss. Can I tell the others it's a go?"

"Okay. When and where?" The man looked so eager Garik couldn't say no.

"I'll request to be your escort—"

"Another guard? I had enough of that back home. Just put the cuffs on. You can lock me to this chair." He put his hands on the arm of a metal chair and waited.

"For a big guy, you have a sense of humor. Come on before someone decides I've kidnapped you." Williams took the door handle, waited until he was certain Garik was with him, and he opened it and stepped outside. A short distance down, two men dressed in a similar fashion met them. Williams pressed himself to the side, said, "Sirs," as they passed, and relaxed once they were gone.

"Aren't you boss of anybody?" Garik teased him.

"You'd think not, wouldn't you? Can you find your way to your quarters from here?"

"I'm free? Seriously?" Garik checked the signs on the walls and knew exactly where he was. "I don't think I'll get lost. Are you certain I don't need a key?"

"Not unless you're heading into any off-limits areas."

"Then I can borrow yours, right?"

"Funny guy. I'll let you know when and where." Williams pivoted on one foot and was gone.

Garik wondered what Devon was up to. No good, he hoped. He cocked his head, listening, then he sniffed. Trees and water, Devon's signature. He could pick it up anywhere.

Follow your nose, Garik. That's what all good wolves can do. Follow your nose.

"MARCO'S HERE?" Garik grinned. "How's the staff liking his marking trick?" Marco Lopez was DNA mated with a lemur, and he had developed a tail and an uncontrollable urge to mark places, items, and people with his distinctive scent.

"And Chad," Devon said. "He's asked about you. Wants to know if you have wings yet, or if you just like coming back to roost in the old hen house."

"He's an idiot." Chad was DNA-matched to a bat, only his transformation had taken him too far. He could only speak through a translator box that could interpret his high-pitched vocalizations. His box made him polite even when he was not.

"Here, someone wants to talk with you." Devon stood, still favoring the leg that had been broken in the car accident, and he called to someone on the other side of the room. "Marina, I've saved you a spot." He pointed and walked away with a grin.

"Garik," she said as she walked up to him. "What big eyes you have!"

"What sexy gills you have." He stood and invited her to join him. Marina Bruni's adaptations were aquatic, originally on one side of her body, but now spreading to both sides. "Have they provided you a place to hydrate?"

"The pool. I swim at night." She smiled, pushing the hair on one side behind her ear, much like her sister Marisa used to do. "I think about you when I'm with Jantzen. He thought so much of you, and I think you did about him."

"You serve as a caregiver for him, right?"

"Not all the time but when I can. I have to hydrate." She shrugged. She could be out of the water for extended times, but only by repeatedly applying high-moisture-content lotions.

"He didn't know me when I arrived." It had stabbed him in the heart, and the memory was nearly as bad.

"Sometimes he seems to remember things. I'm pretty sure he knows me from before, but I'm never certain. Spend time with him. He's the same person, just . . ." Her words trailed off as she searched.

"Incomplete?"

"I will say that is very close." She smiled. "I will see you with him? I feel certain he is in there. Perhaps he knows and cries out to us."

"Perhaps. Thank you, Marina. I will spend some time with him."

He stood as she excused herself. She didn't say where she was headed, but he thought the pool. Some things had been easier for some people in the Bay City facility. This one, while gleaming with newness, hadn't been designed with hybrids in mind.

He wondered what that had to say about their long-term welcome.

He wandered along one wall, touching it in places, looking up to see the ceiling that was like all the other ceilings here. Underground. Covered with dirt. Insulating him from the sun and the sky and whatever weather might come his way. He had begun to dream of trees and dirt and grass and running beneath the moon . . . and this place, no matter how welcoming and protected, was the opposite of all that.

The moon . . . it called to him. To howl? He didn't think so. Just to sit under it, like he used to do with Marisa on the roof of their apartment building. And maybe he would howl, just a little bit.

Just enough to let the moon know that it might be the only one of its kind, but it was never, never alone.

STEPHEN KLANDERMANS, fused with a narwhal for formidable bone regeneration, leaned in and said, "I'll do it."

"Not so fast," Garik cautioned the blond-haired man. His kinky locks were in a tangle of dreads that crashed past his shoulders. The dreads sparkled with medicinal amulets woven into them. "We don't need to break in. I have a key."

"A key?" Stephen smiled. "What about the print lock? How do we get past that?"

"Ever seen one of these?" Garik pulled out a lanyard and attached to it was a keycard.

"Chipped or metallic strip?"

Garik shrugged. "It works, that's all I know." The front said Rory Williams and boasted the man's photo.

"Still getting people in trouble, I see." Stephen reached for the card and looked at the name and the picture. "I know Rory didn't loan this to you."

"He's Rory to you." Garik considered that. It was harder to betray someone who was a friend. He had to trust Stephen in this.

"Drinking buddies. We drink, and he passes out. I remember when I once could." Stephen looked wistful. He hefted the key before holding it out to Garik. "This could make Jantzen's condition worse."

"And it could make him better." Garik had to hope.

"What would Jantzen do? Would he risk everything on a chance? That's what we're doing."

"A good chance. Get me in that lab, and I can repair that sword. Somehow, that sword took something away from Jantzen, and I believe it can give it back to him."

"Said the pied piper of Hamelin. Follow me, children, wherever I go, and I will lead you to fun and games and candy and everything you desire."

"I think you have that mixed with Pinocchio." Garik grinned. "But yeah, if that's what it takes, you, Stephen, can have everything you desire if you go with me tonight."

"Fun and games and candy?" Stephen grinned with enthusiasm.

"Fun and games, anyway. I didn't bring any candy."

"Two out of three ain't bad. An old Meat Loaf song."

"Oldies. I'm always around oldies. Okay, old man, let's get started."

Garik knew exactly where the sword was. Eidetic. Something burned into his brain was there forever, and he never forgot.

This was for Jantzen. *If they won't let me help you, Jantzen, then they'll play by my rules.*

Even if he had to make them up as he went along.

ith Rory's keycard, entering the lab was simple as rolling in new-mown hay. Or howling at the moon on a star-studded night.

Effecting repairs in the intricate machinery of the sword proved much more difficult.

Garik and Stephen found the nighttime corridors in what they had begun to call the Yellowknife Complex empty, but they expected that. This was Canada, land of kindness, trust, and goodwill, where doors were never locked and good behavior was expected because it was, well, *nice*. Once the lights were dimmed, no guards were posted, no cameras blinked red against the ceilings, and it seemed no alarms were set to go off if one of the rare locked doors was unlocked.

It was Canada in the wilderness. Who could find the place, anyway?

Lights revealed the same room Garik had seen earlier, only this time, the sword's casing was open. Large, lighted magnifying glasses on floor stands—now dark—hunched over the sword like greedy insects ready to pluck out and eat the best parts. The schematic diagrams were on the wall, lined up in order, with Garik's hand-drawn one in place at the end, number sixty. Someone with a red pen had made marks on it, adjusting several of Garik's notations. A sticky note attached read, "Must be an error. Look for alternatives."

Garik glanced at the sword as he walked to the wall of schematics. They were all in his head, layered on one another, clear and functioning. Seeing them in print told him more. The reality of the sword came from its physical makeup, not from how his brain organized the conceptual drawings. He had to adjust diodes, reroute capacitors, reset programing. Make sure not to blow up himself and a portion of the complex.

"Can you do this?" Stephen. He stood at the wall and went immediately to the hand-drawn page. He tapped it. "They don't have much confidence."

"I told them." Garik reached for the page and pulled

it from the wall. "I drew it out for them, and still, they can't see it." The thought flashed through him, *only human*, but that was unkind, and he released it. My mind, my thoughts, my way. There was nothing to be gained from unkindness or cruelty.

He would have to remember that when his fury at Rodheimer and Sunchaser once more shifted the world into rainbows . . . if he could find his way through the red-hued landscape of his wolf half's frenzy state and control it.

"So, man, you can do what they can't. I get it. When do we start?" Stephen grinned.

THE LIGHTED magnifying glasses were crucial. Even though Garik could see every detail of the changes needed in his head, they were so tiny in the physical confines of the sword that the work was nearly impossible. He was forced to reference the paper versions over and over, only to face defeat even when he was certain he had done everything exactly as it should be.

Stephen, now sitting off to the side and bouncing a hollow rubber ball he had found off the wall, called out, "Too bad we can't go back and restart the night. Invite some fresh ideas. That's what we need."

"You can't restart—" and Garik's brain clicked with the words, the gears snapping into place, the machine in his head powering up as if it had been stuck in sleep mode. "That's brilliant, Stephen. I should have done that hours ago."

"What's brilliant?" He popped the ball against the wall, and he caught it on its return. Each hit had left a small mark, and one section was nearly black with hits.

"Have I told you about my Street Strider?" Garik was at the wall of schematics, and he searched.

"Your jet-assist bike, sure. What about it?" Smack, the ball hit again.

"It was junk, and the only way to get it to work sometimes was to reset the breakers. I think I've done everything correctly on the sword. I must have. I can see it in my head. I need to find something that would serve as a breaker, something that can reset the entire device."

"Oh, easy." Stephen popped the wall with the ball a final time, caught it, and stood. He walked to one sheet and pointed. "I saw it first thing."

"How . . . do you know . . . this?" Garik studied the symbol he was pointing to. And yes, what he pointed to made sense.

"I'm embarrassed to tell this, but I used to be a techie geek. Not now, but when I was a kid. I studied up on all this, had my parents buy me all sorts of techie stuff. Burned my parents' house down when I was thirteen. Never wanted to mess with it again."

"Interesting. Sure, let's reset the breaker. It works with computers. It's someone's solution, maybe ours."

Garik pulled the schematic from the wall, carried it

to the table, and laid it beside the sword. He moved one of the magnifying glasses and it caught the diagram, making it huge, and he shifted the paper to the side, leaving just the sword under the glass. Each part of the intricate machine appeared outsized, clearly visible, and with Stephen's suggestion, obvious. Garik lifted a tiny pick from the table, and it became a massive lever under the glass. He located the switch, compared it to the diagram, and moved it to the right. It slid too easily, and he wondered whether he had made a mistake. Then he tried to move it back, and it was much harder.

"Trouble?" Stephen breathed down his neck.

"It doesn't want to reengage." He held the pressure on the switch, feeling for a click when it moved.

"I can help there." Stephen bumped Garik's elbow, forcing his hand forward.

"You idiot!" Garik jerked his hand back, and he jabbed an elbow into where he thought Stephen was. The man jumped, and his elbow just grazed him.

"Lucky jump, huh? Did it work?"

"Do you mean did you break it? Likely." Yet, Garik could see that the device was powering up, now emitting a pale blue glow. "Let me reassemble the casing. It seems to be doing something positive."

"Glad I could help." Stephen made his way to his chair and began to throw the ball once more. Thump, catch. Thump, catch. Thump, catch.

TRUST, EVEN in Canada, went only so far, Garik and Stephen found, when Cpl. Rory Williams and a team of fully weaponized soldiers burst into the lab.

"Step back," Williams demanded. "Both of you, hands away from your bodies, touch nothing."

"Oops," Stephen said. "We've been Canadasized."

"You think this is funny? Did you expect to break in here and no one would notice?" Williams, weapon in hand, moved to the table where the completed and fully operational sword glowed, and he lifted his keycard and lanyard. "Each time this is used, the system registers it. I cannot believe you thought you could take this and get away with it. I trusted you, Stephen."

"Me?" Stephen laughed. "You've got the wrong guy."

"Button it. The two of you are in more trouble than you know how to get out of. What have you done to that device? Why is it glowing?" He began to back away.

"It's repaired, I think." Garik lifted an arm, bringing Williams' weapon to bear on him. He lowered the arm. "Okay, I don't want to get shot."

"If you do that fast thing again, my men will shoot to stop you." Williams' gun twitched to tell Garik to keep his distance, and he took a step away from the table.

"So, you're finally the boss of someone."

"You could say that. Right now, I'm the boss of

you." Williams' face looked as dark as it had the day of Garik's arrival. "We're putting you in detention until it can be determined you two have done nothing detrimental to the device. Move towards the door, slowly and with your hands away from your body. Now."

Williams' radio engaged, and he said, "Williams, here." He paused, looked to the table, and said, "Yessir, he has certainly done something with it, and it's now glowing." Another pause, listening, and he continued, "Yessir, the same color our machine uses." Pause. "Acknowledged."

"Not broken?" Garik smiled.

"Not my call. The Major wants to see you and it. Kumar, do we have a way to transport that thing?"

"Um," the man's voice wavered, "I can find something, I'm sure." It was clear he didn't want to touch it.

"You and Bashiir bring it up. We're headed to Theater A."

"Yessir."

OUTSIDE THE lab, Garik saw his mistake. He and Stephen had lost track of time, and the facility was alive with morning traffic. Constructed on one level spreading out under the parking garage and beyond, everyone kept track of everyone else's business by osmosis. What went on permeated the awareness of the occupants, and Garik and Stephen surrounded and marched along under guard drew a crowd, among them, the Bay

City group who immediately recognized him.

"What did you do, Garik?"

"Hey, why is the man being locked away?"

"What's this, another escape?" That was from Chad Sherwin's mechanical translator box. "C'mon, Canadians, where's the smile?"

The Canadians working in the complex moved out of the way, making room for the group of weapons. Kumar and Bashiir brought up the rear of Cpl. Williams' group with the sword atop a wheeled cart.

"Hey, that looks like Sunchaser's sword. Never seen it glow blue before."

"Chris is right. Will you look at that?"

"Look at what?" Dark-haired, bearded Jantzen Hefferly appeared, seeming to step out of nowhere. He normally wandered the corridors without much interference, and this time he put himself in the way of the cart with the glowing sword.

"Pardon, sir." Kumar motioned to Bashiir to hold. "Please, sir, we need to get by."

"I know this." Jantzen seemed to light up with memories. "It . . . I helped create this, then, um, *someone* took it away and claimed it. I . . ." He seemed as puzzled as he was fascinated by the glowing device. He reached out a hand.

"No, Dr. Hefferly. Stand back."

Kumar lifted an arm to block him, but Jantzen was quicker. He placed one hand on the grip, the other on the blade, and he lifted and held it chest high, his eyes glowing with the reflected light from the sword.

Garik's group had stopped at the disruption, and he watched Jantzen with the sword.

"I know how this works," Jantzen murmured, and his hand moved on the hilt, shifting to the pommel.

No one else may have heard him, but Garik's hearing was better than most, and he knew exactly what Jantzen was about to do. With his other hand on the blade, if the sword engaged—

Garik yelled, "No, Jantzen," released the rainbows, and the room swirled. The men with their weapons trained on him had seen the shift in his expression, the compaction in his legs, and watched his throat as the words formed in his vocal cords. They had Cpl. Williams' clear instructions. Shoot if the man does anything untoward. The bullets were on the way before the rainbows could stop them, and Garik's body was pounded by multiple impacts. He staggered as the rainbows vanished, gasping with the pain, wondering if he would survive this time.

Across the room, Jantzen was oblivious, barely glancing away from the sword as the gunfire echoed around him. He engaged the sword, and the blue light brightened and swallowed him. Without warning, he vanished, leaving only wisps of purple smoke in the air, and the sword fell to the floor with a clatter. The casing split, something inside popped and fizzled, and the light faded.

"No!" Garik cried. Jantzen, lost to the sword again, and this time because of him.

"No kidding, you heal quick." Stephen cuffed him on the shoulder. "Your clothes are tattered. Where did the bullets go?"

"It doesn't matter." Dismay, anger at Williams, at Sunchaser, at Rodheimer pummeled Garik. He'd touched the sword, and now he wore Sunchaser's deathmaker mask. He wanted to Houdini out of this place, even the score. He could smell the pines and firs and poplars above ground, and they called to him. Then he pulled himself back to reality. He couldn't smell them at all. He was in here, and they were out there.

Williams nudged him with his weapon. "The Major still wants to see you. Move."

The bullets, he could feel them inside, rubbing, grating on bone with every step. Major Linkletter could do nothing to him now. Nothing that mattered, anyway. Somehow, some way, the people who had trapped him in this life would taste his revenge.

They would face him and see the limits of his anger unleashed. Then they would regret what they had done.

— 10 —

he bed in the detention section laughed at Garik. His body had gifted him another six inches in height, and the bed refused to allow his feet and head on the mattress at the same time. Sometimes, even when you think you're as low as you can go, people can still find something else to take away from you.

He had Stephen's rubber ball, and he tossed it against the wall, catching it when it came back to him. The light was adequate for his night-adapted wolfshine eyes, although most full humans would call it pitch black. Thump, catch. Thump, catch. He noticed a repetitive sound from across the room. He caught the ball, held it, and heard the thunk sound of the ball hitting the wall, then a polite, "I'm caught."

"Chad?"

"In the flesh." The words were spoken by Chad's interpretive translation device that voiced his high-pitched chirps and whistles.

"You can use the light. The switch is by—"

"Don't need it, bush boy." From anyone else, the slur would be harsh and unacceptable. Chad's box interpreted his voice into an invitation for cake and ice cream.

"Right. Echolocation. You know exactly where I am, even in the dark."

"And you, blind as a bat, yes? Why are you chucking that ball in the dark? Practicing midnight bank heist skills?" All said with the purr of polite conversation.

"Why are you bothering me?" Chad was a distraction. Garik's blood still steamed at the major's words: *You have destroyed the very thing we brought you here to save.* And he hadn't mentioned the man the sword took with it even once.

"Came to help you, if you want it."

"How? Echolocation is useless to me. I can see in the dark. You can't walk and have prosthetic arms. Even your voice is fake. What can you do to help me?"

"Ah, and there the big bad wolf is so wrong. The

helpless mouse is the one that chews the rope that sets the captive wolf free."

"Okay, let's hear it." Garik sat up, his feet on the floor, and found Chad just inside the door. He was in his Invacare chair with something on his lap.

"First, this." Chad threw something at him, and Garik caught it. "Ooh, pretty boy. You really can see in the dark."

"A lanyard with a keycard. Williams." Garik glanced up. "This has already gotten me in trouble."

"So, what's a little more? Now this." He pushed the thing off his lap, his prosthetic arms whirring just enough Garik could hear, and it landed with a soft plop on the floor. The chair creaked and shifted, and slowly Chad stood. In the dim light, he looked very much like a normal human with two legs, two arms, and a normal size head. He kicked the package on the floor with the side of his foot. "It's a backpack. I'm not bringing it to you. I've just learned to stand."

"Congratulations. I didn't know you could." Garik reached to pick up the pack, and he felt Chad's hand on his back.

"Hold still. I need to sit."

"Sure." The hand shifted, shook, and shifted again. Then it was gone. Garik set the pack on his bed. "The reason for the demonstration?"

"Standing, people notice me. Sitting? I'm a nothing. Go anywhere, do anything, I'm invisible. People who do see me don't want to notice me, so I hardly ever get questioned. Look in the pack."

Inside, Garik found his passport, driver's license, the rolls of money, everything from the Jeep, including all the food the bag could hold. He pulled out several plant-based items and set them aside. He wouldn't bother with those.

"Are those the cookies?"

"Let me check. Yes."

"Toss them my way. I'll eat them. Here's your plan. At eight, you are to be shipped out to Israel. Linkletter feels you've outstayed your usefulness. Israel wants you for their human-hybrid program. I hear the U.S. version is sweet in comparison. At two every morning, this complex opens the vents above ground to replenish its air. It's one-thirty. You have thirty minutes. Don't come back this time. If any of us deserves freedom, it's you."

"Come with me." Garik offered, but he knew it was impossible. How could Chad survive out there?

"Sweet but no. Rodheimer took care of that. Make him pay. That's better than freedom for me."

Garik's eyes misted, and by the time he had them cleared, he was alone. It was time to move.

BOOTS. C'MON, Chad, you couldn't give me boots? Dawn was lighting the eastern sky behind him, and as far as he could see, the glimmer of water said the ground would be boggy for a long time to come.

A road. He needed a road, just not one close to the complex. He had no idea if anyone would be out looking for him, and the more lost he was, the harder he would be to find. He couldn't stay lost forever, but for a time, the trees, the dirt and grass and water. He wanted it all, and he never wanted to go south again.

He'd be back. The wilderness called him. It never had before, but now, he knew it was his home ... would be his home, as soon as he evened the score for what had been taken from him.

A WEEK and a half of mud and sun and sleeping on the damp ground convinced Garik that the highway was a better option. The chance of being spotted was worth the risk. A trucker provided a ride for ten hours before pulling over, telling him he was welcome to stick with him, but he had to pay for his own meal and sleep in the back. Another five hours on the road, he put on his blinker for Vancouver, and Garik bid him farewell.

The border just south of Vancouver was a concern. His pack of money had thinned, and if his passport was flagged, where did that leave him? He breathed easier in Blaine, Washington, somewhere he'd never visited. A place to spend the night, shower, and wash his clothes consumed most of what was left, and he looked for help signs in storefronts and along the road. A kennel advertised DOG WALKER WANTED. Hungry, he pushed open the door and was employed for the first time in his life.

No worries. The dogs loved him. The sun was bright, and the kennel had a spare room at the back if he would also clean the cages in the mornings.

Five weeks later, summer was rolling in strong, and he was on the road again. Trucks rumbled past on the highway: with covers; open; rigs with long cradles of logs; none willing to take him along.

It was time to change the rules and take what no one wanted to give him. He needed a truck with a bed he could access but with cover for protection. He had over thirty seconds now, nearly forty-five, still a slim margin when doing something dangerous. Two rigs rolled by, the backs revealing metal doors. He could break through, but this wasn't about damaging something that wasn't his, rather about borrowing what someone else wasn't using.

Then a canvas-sided truck appeared. The heavy, vinyl fabric flexed in the wind, battering whatever was inside. A section at the back flexed more than the rest, and Garik decided to take it. He turned up the rainbows full force. The clouds stilled themselves, the trees no longer swayed in the wind, and the vehicles on the highway were very near frozen. As Garik ran toward the truck, the wheels inched forward at a snail's pace. He counted as he ran, eleven, twelve. He leaped up on the back bumper to untie the flap, sixteen, seventeen.

He found the empty space, barely enough for him and his backpack, twenty-one, twenty-two. He slipped his pack off his back and worked it into the space, twenty-six, twenty-seven. He found a handhold and pulled himself up, thirty-one, thirty-two. He didn't really fit, but by adjusting the pack under his legs, he would survive, thirty-six, thirty-seven. He reached for the fastener and tried to get it to latch, forty-two, forty-three, but failed. The rainbows slipped away from him. The vinyl fabric now buffeted in the wind, creating a drumming sound that battered his ears. Not the best he could have asked for, but he'd take what he could get. He let himself drift into the upper edges of exhaustion, his margins trimmed about as close as he dared.

TWO RIDES later and three long nights of walking, and he could see the top of Corona Tower through the trees. He'd taken to doing that, riding when he could, but doing his walking at night. The stars, the moon, the smell of the dirt and grass and trees. It felt more home than he ever remembered the city being. Underground, how had he stood it?

Part of the change was him. He could hear a cricket in the woods and know if it was male or female and whether it was healthy enough to make a good snack if his food sources ran low. Squirrels, snakes, rabbits, all were out there, and he could hear the differences in each one.

His sense of smell, too. He wanted to pick up sticks just to breathe in their aromas. Nuts, berries, they were layered in information about the season, how much rain had fallen, even other animals that had come by, leaving a reminder of themselves.

He'd found he could tolerate plant-based foods to a degree, but meat was his preference. Often, he would purchase a burger and toss the bun. It was little more than cardboard to him.

His body had changed, too. His guard hairs were denser, prickling his back when the wind caught his shirt. He hadn't looked, but he knew what he'd find, and he wore long sleeves buttoned at the wrists and his collar pulled close to his neck. The backs of his hands, no one could miss that. And when he cleared his throat, like as not it came out a growl. Did it mean anything? Christian could answer that if he hadn't been harvested for parts.

He veered from the highway when he approached Bay City, finding his way into the forested area east of the industrial park. The hills rose to almost mountainous proportions, and he could see the bay out beyond The Docks and Harbor Shipyards. Waldorf's Department Store was hidden by tree-shrouded Shady Ridge Acres, an exclusive residential enclave just north of Ninth, but the flags at Argyle Station on the west side of town flapped in the breeze. It was nice to know someone was hoisting them and taking them down each day. Not everything in the city had broken down with the disaster that had terrorized his home.

A tornado of terror, the second worst thing Garik had ever endured.

Seeing Marisa buried under the falling storefront had been the worst. Then, the rioting, the stores burned, Marisa's family losing The Flower Shop where she had died. They had given up two daughters to Bay City and Corona Tower. He hoped they moved on to find a happier place to live. He didn't see how they could remain here. Everything would remind them of what they had lost.

He began his journey through the trees, the twigs breaking under his feet, the boots purchased in Blaine battered with the miles he'd traveled. He longed for a moment for his old bedroom at his aunt's apartment. He let the feeling go almost as quickly. She had moved on to Arik even before Garik left. Boyfriends can be lovers, nephews only friends.

He missed Marisa. Being back to Bay City flooded her memory over him. He wanted to reach out to her, do what he should have done then: told her how he felt, taken her hand, kissed her.

Who was that Garik, anyway? A child, a boy, a teen, a youth with unformed dreams and little ambition. He'd loved skating and his jet-assist bike. Nothing else had mattered. In a year it had vanished, gone, a dandelion blown apart in the wind.

He reached First, and he turned left. He passed Bay City Medical with its fancy entry gates and landscaped grounds. Cars and more cars, as if the lifeblood of the city flowed once more, oblivious to the damage that Corona Tower had caused in his life. At Coolidge, he looked south, the direction of the warehouse Dieter's father had converted into an indoor skate park. The passcode might still work. Nine blocks. It was worth a chance.

Garik hiked his backpack higher on his shoulders, looked uphill along Coolidge's unbending length, took in the red lights from First to Norfleet, and attempted to recall the graffiti he had once known on every building from Meyers south to Buda. As he walked, he tried to draw each one in his mind, surprised at how hard it was.

Then, he hadn't been wolf boy then . . . werewolf . . . lougarou . . . demon spawn . . . Frankenstein. He was all of those now, and more.

He had received a perfect memory. Eidetic. When he saw the graffiti images this time, he would own them forever.

— 11 —

ow many months since he and Muhammad and Ibn had skated the ramps in Dieter's indoor park?

The passcode was good, the water on—and power. Likely Deiter's father had taken a year's lease, and when he had run with his son from the disaster in the Tower's basement, the rest of the lease was wasted.

Except not the previous night. Garik had enjoyed a bathroom, the small kitchenette, and a place to sleep insulated from the world. And it hadn't cost him any of his dwindling stash of cash.

He dropped off the halfpipe to the floor and looked underneath for an extra board. There had been several when he was here last, and he didn't expect they had been moved. Four, and he looked through them, all high-end boards, trucks, and wheels, just what he would expect from a man who would rent his son a warehouse just to build him an indoor skate park. He picked one with a sunflower on the top and Rock It! on the bottom. Father sun and mother earth. He carried it up the narrow steps to the top of the pipe and twirled it, one end in his hand and the other balanced on the loft's wooden surface. He pictured himself floating on the board, a handplant, the thrill, but he wore his boots from Blaine, and none of the shoes from under the pipe were sized for his feet, the penalty he paid for his phenomenal growth over the past year. He released the board into the pipe without him and watched it roll down, then back and forth until it came to a rest at the bottom. Even this was lost to him. He jumped into the pipe, a clean and easy leap into the center, landing just beside the board. He picked it up, returned it to its place under the pipe, and gathered his pack.

The Tower was waiting. It was time to make his peace. He looked around the space, a bit wistful for the friends he had seen here for the final time. Where were they now? Muhammed and Ibn were finishing up their senior year of school. John Carter was left on the parking garage floor, dead as far as he knew. Alyna, Amy,

Marco. And Justin in Canada. Christian never made it this far, and Jantzen. He had been here that night. Garik's eyes burned for Jantzen, lost twice, the second time his fault. If he'd never touched the sword, never seen that final page of schematics, never tried to fix what he didn't know how to fix.

The memories reignited his anger, and it simmered just under his skin. He checked his pack, making sure he was prepared. Paul Gberie had suggested fruit bars. Garik had stocked up on beef sticks. The better to chew on, my dear. He could laugh at the old fairy tale. His plan was to walk to the Tower, and with beef sticks in hand, he would entangle the place with rainbows, shedding beef stick wrappers along the way, whatever it took to bring down Rodheimer and Sunchaser.

They didn't know about the rainbows, which meant it would work. It had to. It was the only plan he had to play.

THE DAY BEFORE, walking along Coolidge, he had studied the graffiti on the west side of the street. This morning, he took in the east. It was the last time he would walk this street, and he wanted to absorb the energy and fractured beauty of Uptown. He turned on First, walked west for three blocks and crossed the powerline right-of-way to Park Avenue before heading north towards Central Park. The burned cars were gone, but the charred asphalt mocked the city's efforts to make the past year disappear. The police department headquarters building was freshly scrubbed, and new paint covered part of the structure. Several store windows along his walk were filled in with plywood, painted with bright colors or murals to disguise the empty and blackened spaces hiding inside. The walls of one of the big houses in Pill Hill still stood, but its roof was missing. An overhanging tree was dead, its late-spring branches bare of leaves, killed by the heat of the flames.

Corona Tower dominated the sky long before he reached its base, a black fist that had smashed into him and crushed him. Now it was time for him to crush back. He walked with determined steps as he approached Rock Island, the street that would lead him to the back entrance of the Tower. He turned, his view a straight shot, expecting to see the scar left when the parking garage was bombed by Marisa and was surprised to see a nearly complete garage to replace it.

Even Marisa, her final fingerprint on the Tower, wiped away as if she'd never lived.

Nothing else. They would not have the chance to take anything else from him.

THE ENTRANCE to the garage was blocked with wood-and-fiberglass sawhorses, but the inside appeared fully functional, with gates and payment stiles in place. Garik leaped the sawhorses, easy as pie, and loped up the ramp leading to the Stamford Suites entrance where he would likely find Gunther Diehl. The concierge had always treated him kindly, and he didn't want him to suffer. He hoped he stayed out of his way. If Garik's plan worked, the man wouldn't see him until the damage to Rodheimer and Sunchaser was already done.

Through the glass doors into the Tower's lobby, it seemed business as usual. Charity Cellers at her desk. Choi Bak with a luggage cart, stopping to pull a cloth from his hip pocket to wipe down the brass rails on the cart before rolling it into a recess along the wall.

Wait, Garik, wait, he told himself, as he squatted and leaned with his back against a recess framed by two concrete columns. He didn't have a passkey, and to enter by force was to warn them. His retribution must come as a surprise. Someone would open the door. In five minutes, an hour. He had waited for weeks. He could wait half a day more.

BY NOON he realized the garage might not be his way inside. No one was using the door, in or out. Then Boris Lindemann of all people walked toward the door with a small dog on a leash. Boris lived in the Tower in Stamford Suites. He likely took his dog out every day. He pushed open the door without a passkey and stepped inside the garage just far enough to let the door close behind him. He studied his watch, tapped it several times, then pulled out a phone and began to talk. When the dog was finished, Boris reached for the door, opened it, and made his way inside . . . without a key!

"Hours wasted," Garik muttered as he stepped out of the shadows and shouldered his backpack. He sorted a handful of the beef sticks into various pockets. Ten beef sticks gave him ten minutes. Twenty meant twenty minutes. He had a hundred with him. He figured he would be sick of beef sticks before he was finished, but that would give him an hour and a half of revenge.

He unzipped his anger as he stepped to the glass doors, letting his bottled fury batter at time, breaking into the shell of now and then and in a minute. *Marisa, John, Paul.* The anger bled from him, fueling the elation of his rising frenzy. *Jantzen, dead twice, and at his own hand.* Garik became two people, the youth—now a man—who had loved and lost. He could admit that now. Jantzen, his mentor, the man who had stepped in to save him, to become a father to him. Garik was also wolf, what the Tower had made him, no longer completely human, if human at all. Which would win in the end?

Garik wrested the rainbows from nothingness, controlled the rising tide around him by sheer will, a tornado vortex of colors twisting into every nook and cranny, turning the glass into shimmering, transparent rock candy, the door handles into glowing unicorn horns, and the lobby of the tower on the other side into a cascade of light, with color dripping from every surface.

He was through the doors, the air sucking in after him in a vortex of red, green, and violet, searching, searching, needing to find the people who had brought him to this. *Where are you? Where are you?* Gunther Diehl to the right, standing at his desk, lifting a sheet of paper, his eyes turned toward the private Stamford Suites elevator as if it had just dinged to indicate a passenger about to disembark. Color turned Gunther into a glowing lollipop, ready for Garik's anger to consume. Yet, Gunther wasn't his target, and Garik searched elsewhere.

Deeper into the lobby, the ornate sculptures, the elaborate furniture groupings, and people! Many people sitting here, visiting there, children in strollers, all alight in rainbow colors. They surprised Garik as he counted thirty-four, thirty-five, and his first wrapper fluttered from his fingertips and into the wasteland of real time, no longer enveloped in his vortex of speed.

Past Charity Cellers, leaving the woman mired in an easter egg cacophony of pink and yellow and blue; and the elevator, the door partially open and someone's hand reaching through. Color swirled out, tumbling onto the lobby floor into a liquid pool of effervescent time, colder and harder the faster Garik moved.

A second wrapper fluttered into real time, taking on its own little rainbow, frozen in a pool of light. Garik left it behind in his search, forgotten on his way to exact his revenge. He approached the door of the Director's office, with swirls of color leaking from the edges, blurring the name on the front. Still, he remembered Major Kennedy leading him inside, the tirade launched at him as he stood between Weston Rodheimer and Colonel Brace, becoming the center of their attack, and Brace's threats against Marisa's family before he was finally released.

Garik burned hot, another wrapper gone, and he wanted to lean against the door, feel it bow under the pressure of his shoulder, the satisfying crack as it gave way to his superior force. They would know he was no longer the boy they had trapped in this changing body, the timid youth who cowered when they threatened, the high school student no one would miss because he wasn't worth considering in Bay City's scheme of reckoning.

Yet, yet.

Garik turned, taking in what he hadn't yet absorbed. The people. A sign saying Welcome to Corona Tower. A new casualness to the furniture groupings. Sculptures that had been replaced with city-friendly designs, one of a life-size skater boy in bronze, his right hand holding the edge of a halfpipe, his feet pulled up under him, his left on a board floating beside him. The skater, a tangle of hair tied at the nape of his neck, now coming loose and flying free . . . the facial structure . . . familiar in a way that only a man who had once viewed that face in a mirror could know.

Garik forced his eyes away, tried to remember why his pockets bulged, and touched a beef stick. Eat, energy, it's time; and he opened one and released the wrapper as he searched for a way . . . and came up with nothing. He withdrew behind a grouping of small trees in one corner and fell back into real time. The groupings of people in the lobby were instantly boisterous, cheerful and friendly. Gunther set his paper down and smiled as a white-haired woman exited the Stamford Suites elevator. Charity stood and called a greeting to Choi Bak. The main elevator fully opened, and the hand became an arm, a person, a couple, and a family. Then out stepped Jantzen Hefferly.

Garik collapsed to the floor, his back hitting the wall hard, and his pack sliding up and off one shoulder. It was nothing to him against seeing the man he had come to vindicate walking into the room whole and alive. How? His mind clicked, the gears turned . . . gather, evaluate, extrapolate . . . the paths of probabilities painted themselves on the lobby floor, the opportunities he could choose, could walk, could cast aside, the branches that would evaporate as he made those choices.

It had to be the sword, not broken. Repaired! He had repaired it, and it had worked! Always, Jantzen had reformed from his gaseous state into himself whole and undamaged. Why would this time be any different? He put his hand to the floor to stand, to call out to him, and heard Jantzen begin an address to the group in the lobby.

"Welcome, Citizens of Bay City. Corona Tower has been part of this city for many years, but I consider this to be our true opening day. The recent upset to our city is behind us, and Corona Tower guarantees its continued support of our beloved Bay City through healthcare initiatives and projects to maintain and improve the city's park system and more. As a pledge of the changes at Corona Tower, it's time we opened our facility to you. Bay City is our home, and we want you to share in the rebirth of Bay City and Corona Tower. Enjoy today's events."

Outside the windows, a massive release of colorful balloons, a rainbow of a different sort, brought oohs and aahs from the people. Garik was speechless. This violated everything he knew, and he watched as the paths in front of him narrowed to one.

Jantzen. He was the only one who could explain.

— 12 —

our plans?" Jantzen quizzed Garik as they exited the elevator into the subterranean warrens of Corona Tower's massive underground research center.

"My plans?" Garik laughed sourly. "I have no plans, except to return here and exact revenge on the two people I've come to hate most in my life. And now, you've taken even that from me."

"Is that a bad thing?" Jantzen was kind, warm, and seemed to want to engage with Garik, reconnect, renew some level of their earliest relationship. "I'm in the penthouse now that Weston is no longer part of the organization. My old apartment can still be yours. I've kept it vacant, hoping you would return."

"I saw the sculpture."

"Yes." Jantzen glanced away and ran his hand over his hair. "Does it bother you?"

"No. That's not me any longer." He pictured Dieter's warehouse that morning. He'd tried to regain that part of him, and it had already slipped away, gone forever. "What happened to Halo Sunchaser?"

"South Africa happened to her. Her brother Bongani is in the government, and when he discovered she was part of our program, he immediately recalled her."

"So, she got away scot-free."

"Hardly." Jantzen chuckled. "She will face worse penalties there than I could ever impose on her. Weston might be facing a trial for abuse, cruelty, and improper use of government funds, but he can rest easy that it's the U.S. government after him and not the South African one."

"And Colonel Brace. Protected by his own."

"That's life." He shrugged. "But the reason we're down here. Follow me."

The activity area. Memories, no longer quite real, attached themselves to every wall, every chair, everything they passed. Then they approached the glass-walled pool Marina had shown him the first day he had been able to get out and about. It was empty then. It wasn't now.

"Marina?" Garik stepped to the glass, pressed his hands to it. Inside, a beauty with layers of glistening scales, pulsing gills, and long black hair turned his direction.

"Garik." The words came from a speaker in the ceiling, but it was Marina's voice.

"You came back. I didn't expect to see you here." He smiled. She looked so much like Marisa, her expressive eyes, dainty chin, the smile that did something to him inside. "You are beautiful. Does anyone ever tell you that?"

"Yes, just now. And did you see this?" She pointed to the sides of her neck, her gills pulsing, the water creating small ripples of light on the pool floor.

"That's what makes you beautiful." He wanted to ask if she was lonely, if anyone ever swam with her. He could, let his lungs fill with water, his aquatic part of his body's ability to adapt to any environment . . . and live underground without the sun and sky and trees and dirt. "I'm glad to see you happy. Keep changing. You are more beautiful each time I see you."

"Thank you. You, also, are changing. Marisa would be proud of you. Her love from me to you." She placed one hand against his, the glass the barest of separation, and after a moment, she smiled and pushed away, gracefully withdrawing into another world.

"Come," Jantzen said, one hand on Garik's shoulder. "Let's head back upstairs. I want to know how you evaded us for nearly two months. We were notified when you crossed back into the States, but then you disappeared again."

"Mud, rain, living a dog's life." He shrugged it off. He remembered Cpl. Williams' bullets and his body expelling them during those weeks. It was an experience he'd rather forget.

"A dog's life." Jantzen nudged him. "That's funny. We contacted Yellowknife the next morning, and you were already gone. We scoured the highways, everywhere. You simply vanished. A dog's life."

"Seriously. I walked dogs for five weeks in Blaine." They were at the elevator, and Garik noticed Jantzen didn't use a passkey. The new Tower, all free and open to everyone.

"Then that's why we didn't find you south of the border. We had no idea you would stay there. You must have been totally off grid. You didn't pop up anywhere."

"I lived in the kennel. They had a room in the back I could use if I cleaned the cages. Of course, I'm half dog. Who else would want me?"

"About that." The elevator doors closed them in. "You will stay? Anywhere, my old apartment, anywhere in the basements, you choose. The penthouse—" longingly "—has plenty of room for two if that appeals to you. I remember some of my time in Canada, you showing up—"

"Do you really?" Garik remembered the blank looks. "You weren't there, not even a fragment of you. I tried to engage you, and you had to ask someone if you had my name right. This place—" He pictured Devon, the recreation director who had become his friend. Devo . . . Devon-o . . . *right-o, Devon-o* . . . and he smiled.

"What's the smile for?"

"A friend." He watched the elevator numbers click over. Without noticing, the car had carried them to the top of the Tower, no passkey required. "I need outside, Jantzen. Not any of this. Not the windows, not the views, not this city. You people changed me." He noticed his terminology. Jantzen no longer felt like *us* but had become *them*. Jantzen wanted all this. Garik didn't. He was no longer the youth that craved a mentor. He had become what he was supposed to be, a man who needed his freedom, independence, and to figure out how to make his life work without someone standing over his shoulder.

The doors opened into the penthouse, the glass walls, the expansive views. The furniture was the same, something Garik saw as Jantzen's link to his childhood friend. Weston Rodheimer might have trashed their relationship, but Jantzen would always be intermingled with the man he had once been intimately bonded to.

Garik walked to the glass wall looking toward the

water, the sun catching the waves and calling to him. *Freedom, Garik. Just one glass wall away. Step through. I'm here, ready to take you anywhere your dreams lead you.* He turned. "I need to go home."

"This is your home. I'll give you this place and move back into my old one. Whatever you want."

"No, *home.*" Trees, dirt, grass, sky. Outside, the smells and sounds. He realized his time on the road, walking during the nights, that was who he was. Not this, not carpets and chairs and windows. He was beyond that. The realization welled up in him. Beyond human, beyond boyhood crushes on men who could melt into purple vapor. Such tricks no longer fascinated him. He had earned enough of his own, and they had done nothing except steal away the things he held most dear in his life.

"Where is home for you?" Jantzen approached, then stopped before he reached him.

"I watched you die twice, Jantzen." Garik looked out the window again, not wanting to see the reactions on the man's face. He had needed Jantzen to want him, to treat him like a son, to need to spend time with him as much as Garik had needed him. "The first time I blamed it on Sunchaser. The second time I blamed it on me. I repaired the sword, and you picked it up, not knowing it was repaired, and you turned it on. You vanished, and the sword was broken. How was I supposed to handle that? I had become the murderer."

He whispered, "I had become Sunchaser."

"I wanted . . . had hoped . . ." Jantzen hesitated, his eyes fixated beyond the glass, then he took a deep breath and his voice shifted to a brighter, more positive tone. "Perhaps Canada? Do you want to return to the facility there? I'm sure Major Linkletter would invite you back. Or Israel. Their programs are running down avenues we haven't considered. Lt. Wilder has extended an offer to open negotiations with the Israelis on your behalf—"

"Canada." The memories of the forests and the wild outdoors were like fresh air on his tongue. Yet, he knew the realities of being in a foreign country. Canada, also, could never be home. "Not Israel. I need trees and growing things, more than they can provide." And they had offered to take him already, likely to cut him up for research.

"I can arrange Canada for you. Yellowknife, anywhere. What do you need from me?"

"My freedom. To cut the cords."

"You will carry a phone? Call? To lose you—"

"No phone. Just me. Alaska, perhaps. Mining, logging, maybe the oil fields. Just outside. That's where I need to be."

"Let me set that up for you. I can arrange the company jet to get you there—"

"You're not getting it." Garik thrust his hands deep in his pockets, his newly grown nails biting his palms, his voice taking an edge. "No cords, no help, just me. I'm not the kid who needs looking after any longer. I need to make it on my own."

"I deserved that." Jantzen stepped up to stand beside Garik, looking out, a margin of space between them. "My apologies. You are yourself, one hundred percent, and you have the right to live your life without me or anyone looking over your shoulder. I should have seen that before."

"I appreciate what you've done for me—" Garik wanted to trust Jantzen's words. Freedom, release, acceptance. Would the man follow through? *Could* he?

"Just don't do it anymore, right?"

"You mentored me though this. I couldn't have done it without you. At one point, I looked at you as my father—"

"Hey," Jantzen cautioned. "I'm not a graybeard yet. Don't give me crutches before I earn them."

Garik laughed, glad to see Jantzen teasing again. "Friend, then. Acceptable?" He truly liked the man, at one point admitted he might have loved him, but he had grown past him. Still, he didn't wish to hurt him.

"I'll take whatever I can get. When are you leaving?"

"A few days. Visit with Marina, see if there's anyone else in the city I might like to say goodbye to."

"Your aunt. She's still here."

"Iri." Garik considered the situation. "Not if she's

with Arik."

"Done, if you'll let me do that for you."

"It won't change my mind. No cords, Jantz."

"Understood."

Garik didn't reply. He read the emotions behind the word in the man's heartbeat, his pheromones, the longing emanating from him. As Jantzen had taught him, you shouldn't give away everything you can do, especially when it would hurt a friend, one Garik had already left behind.

THE BIG DAY arrived a week later, the middle of May, with sunshine and wispy clouds in the sky. Garik sat in the penthouse lacing up new hikers, in heavy jeans and a flannel shirt. It was warm in Bay City, but where he was going, he expected winter year-round.

Backpack. Tent. The whole nine yards, Jantzen's gift to him. He stood, faced Jantzen, and said, "It's time."

"One last thing." Jantzen pulled out a slim leather wallet. He opened it to reveal a metal card inside, then closed it and held it out to Garik.

"I don't want that." Garik looked away and reached for his backpack.

"No limits. You don't have to use it, but if you need it . . . any amount. The card never expires."

"I won't use it."

"You won't take a watch or a phone—"

"I don't want to be tracked."

"I understand. This one thing, though. Emergencies only. Bus fare, plane fare, or buy the whole plane. This card will allow it. Carry it. For me."

"For you." Garik considered the card. "I want to disappear, Jantzen. Gone forever. That card can track me."

"Only if you use it, and only I will know."

That you're safe, but Jantzen hadn't needed to say that. Garik understood. He held out his hand, stroked the leather, and slid it into a pouch in his pack.

"Then I'm gone. North, somewhere. You'll be able to track when I cross the border, but don't. Please."

Garik hiked his pack and slipped it on, and he walked to the elevator without looking back. Making his way across the mall, he looked back at the Tower, wondering what had fascinated him about it for so long. It was a building, steel and glass. Where he was heading was so much better.

He faced east into the rising sun. A day's walk and he would turn north. How long until he got there? It didn't matter.

He had all the time in the world.

Enjoy our Omnibus Edition containing all ten books.

The Human-Hybrid Project
Omnibus Edition
The Human-Hybrid Project

You've enjoyed each book in this series, or you've started with Book 10 and want to experience the rest of the story. The Omnibus Edition allows you to have all ten books at your fingertips. At approximately 270,000 words, *The Human-Hybrid Project, Omnibus Edition*, is available in digital, paperback, and hardcover format.

Available on Amazon

The Human-Hybrid Project

Addictive!

A 10-book series you won't be able to forget. Explore each upcoming book, the characters, and more at www.thehumanhybridproject.com.

Book 1   Book 2

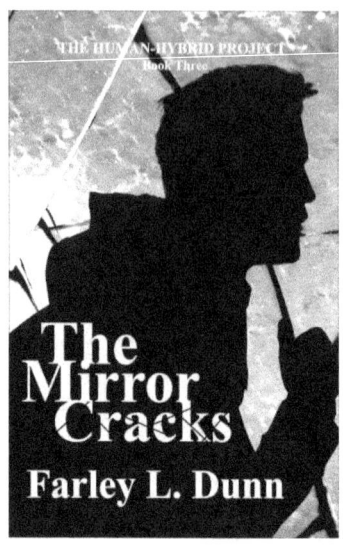

Book 3

Book 4

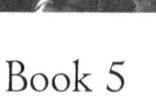

Book 5

Book 6

Book 7   Book 8

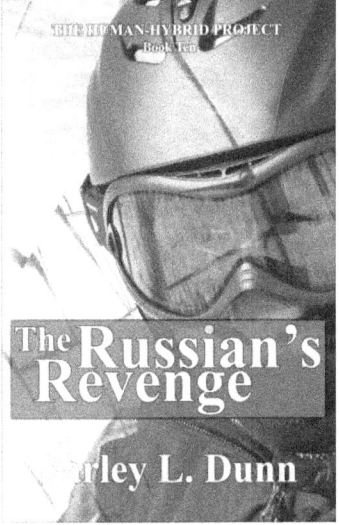

Book 9   Book 10